W9-BPO-399

SOMEWHERE OFF THE COAST OF MAINE

Focusing on novels with contemporary concerns, Bantam New Fiction introduces some of the most exciting voices at work today. Look for these titles wherever Bantam New Fiction is sold:

WHITE PALACE by Glenn Savan

SOMEWHERE OFF THE COAST OF MAINE by Ann Hood

COYOTE by Lynn Vannucci (on sale in July)

VARIATIONS IN THE NIGHT by Emily Listfield (on sale in August)

LIFE DURING WARTIME by Lucius Shepard (on sale in September)

THE HALLOWEEN BALL by James Howard Kunstler (on sale in October)

BANTAM NEW FICTION

SOMEWHERE
OFF THE
COAST OF MAINE

ANN HOOD

BANTAM BOOKS
TORONTO · NEW YORK · LONDON · SYDNEY · AUCKLAND

SOMEWHERE OFF THE COAST OF MAINE
A Bantam Book / July 1987

Library of Congress Cataloging-in-Publication Data

Hood, Ann.
  Somewhere off the coast of Maine.

  I. Title.
PS3558.0537S6 1987   813'.54   86-47900
ISBN 0-553-34382-3

       Published simultaneously in the United States and Canada

---

Bantam Books are published by Bantam Books, Inc. Its trademark, consisting
of the words "Bantam Books" and the portrayal of a rooster, is Registered
in U.S. Patent and Trademark Office and in other countries. Marca Registrada.
Bantam Books, Inc., 666 Fifth Avenue, New York, New York 10103.

PRINTED IN THE UNITED STATES OF AMERICA

FG   0 9 8 7 6 5 4 3 2 1

For my parents,
with love

ACKNOWLEDGMENTS

A very special thanks to William Decker, Nicholas Delbanco, Maxine Groffsky, Melissa Hood, Carrie Kronish, Glenn Russow, Bob Reiss, Jane Silva, Joshua Ziff, and, especially, Deb Futter.

SOMEWHERE OFF THE COAST OF MAINE

PART ONE

BEYOND THE PICTURES

SPARROW, 1984

To Sparrow, her father was a man standing in front of a Day-Glo green VW van in a picture dated June 1969. The picture had been taken the year before Sparrow was born. In it, her father's hair was bushy and blond and he had a big droopy moustache. Sparrow liked the way he was looking up, with his head tilted back and his mouth open in a wide smile.

Sparrow's mother, Suzanne, never talked about Sparrow's father. Suzanne was a serious businesswoman. She dressed in pleated skirts and Oxford shirts with little bow ties. She would tell Sparrow to forget about the past and look ahead. "Don't worry," she would say, "about things that happened a long time ago." Sparrow's obsession with her father began to grow when her mother started to date Ron.

Sparrow found the picture of her father in an old poetry book of her mother's. She'd been looking for a poem to read aloud in English class. The picture fell out when she opened the book and as soon as Sparrow saw it, she knew it was Him. She studied it for a long time, searching for some resemblance—the nose, maybe, or around the mouth. She said his name out loud. Abel. Finally, she took the picture to her mother.

"This is him, isn't it?" she demanded as she put the picture down in front of her mother.

Suzanne was getting ready for a dinner-date with Ron. She was wearing a white slip and sitting at her vanity table applying makeup. The table was littered with brushes, creams, and pots of powdery colors. The room smelled like Chanel No. 5.

Her mother looked down at the picture and for a moment Sparrow thought she was going to faint. Her face grew pale under her perfectly blended Gingerberry blush. But, almost immediately, she regained her usual professional demeanor.

"Where did you get that?" She avoided looking at Sparrow or the picture. Instead, she concentrated on lining her eyes in kohl.

"I was looking for a poem to read in English class and I pulled out a copy of *Howl* and it fell out. It's him, isn't it?" she demanded again.

"*Howl?* That's not a book for a fourteen-year-old. As I recall, there are a lot of homosexual references and . . . and it's very . . . um . . . drug-oriented."

"You told me that you didn't have any pictures of him."

"I have some lovely poems that you can bring to class. Classic ones. Robert Frost, for instance. I have a beautiful collection of his poetry. He wrote about the woods and nature. Very lovely poems."

"Mother," Sparrow said angrily. Below them, boats sailed in Boston Harbor. She could hear the whistle of the ferry returning from Cape Cod.

Suzanne put the eye pencil down, sighed, and picked up the picture.

"I didn't think I had any pictures of him. He kept all that sort of thing. Honestly, one forgotten picture in some silly book and you act as if I'm withholding state's evidence." She turned her gaze toward Sparrow now. One eye was neatly outlined in black, the other was untouched, giving the impression that one eye was either unusually large or unusually small.

"I never knew what he looked like," Sparrow said.

Suzanne opened her mouth as if to reply. But instead, she looked back down at the photograph and studied it closely, fingering the outline of the van. She shook her head. "It looks so strange," Suzanne said.

Sparrow waited for her to say something else. Like, "I remember the day that picture was taken" or "I wonder if he still has that moustache." But she just kept staring at the picture, then put it back down.

"I don't look very much like him, I guess," Sparrow said, and picked up the photo. Her hair was a darker blond, more like Suzanne's. But her eyes, Sparrow thought, had flecks of the same green as his.

"Why won't you tell me about him?"

Her mother began to outline her other eye.

"Mom?" Sparrow noticed her mother's hand was shaking slightly.

"It's not healthy to dwell on things like this. To relive them over and over again."

"Relive them?" Sparrow said. "I don't even remember living them."

"You know what?" Suzanne said, her hand steadier now. "Bring in that Robert Frost book and we'll go through it together. You're going to be surprised when you see how much I know about poetry. In fact, you'll be stunned. I'm a real poetry whiz."

Sparrow didn't answer. The thing you're really a whiz

at, she thought, is changing the subject. This subject, anyway.

"I just want to know what he's like," Sparrow said. "That's all."

"No, you don't," Sparrow thought her mother mumbled.

"What? What did you say?"

Suzanne looked at her again, both eyes neatly lined now.

" 'Stopping by the Woods on a Snowy Evening' is a lovely poem. Really lovely. And it's much more appropriate for class. You'll see."

Sparrow had the picture for three months. She studied it often, not really certain what it was she expected to find there. At night, in the dark, she called it to mind in perfect detail—the lime green of the van, the wide smile and tilted head. She could almost hear the laughter.

Her mother and Ron saw each other almost every night. He always brought Sparrow little presents. A small box of Godiva chocolates. An African violet in a tiny green pot. A pin with her initials engraved on it. Sparrow threw them all away.

For the past year or so, Sparrow's mother called her Susan. She said that the name Sparrow was too dated, too silly. For a time, her mother explained, everyone named their children Summer or Sunshine. "If you had been a boy," her mother said, "I would have named you something like Sage." Sparrow asked her mother if she were a boy, would she be called Steve all of a sudden? "No one will take you seriously with a name like Sparrow." Sparrow hated being called Susan. Whenever her mother called her that, she refused to answer. "You didn't think it was silly when I was born, did you? Why did you name me that if you thought it was so silly?"

Sparrow's mother shook her head. "It doesn't matter," she said, sounding almost sad.

Sparrow played the piano in a trio. They had practice every Thursday after school. The school was in Cambridge, a pair of old brick mansions that sat across from each other. At lunch or study period the girls would walk down to the Charles and watch the Harvard crew team practice. When Ron told Sparrow that he'd been on the Harvard crew team "back in the Stone Age," she stopped going to watch. Instead, she'd sit alone and read, determined not to waste her time drooling over a dozen potential Rons sculling.

One of the girls in the trio, the flutist, lived around the corner from the school. Sparrow and Blair, the violinist, lived in the city, and had to wait for rides home after practice. Their parents were supposed to take turns picking them up, but Blair's father ended up doing it more because Suzanne was always getting detained at the office. Once, to Sparrow's horror, her mother sent Ron to get them. The two girls sat in the backseat. Sparrow stared out the window the whole time and Blair poked her whenever Ron said something. Don't you ever, Sparrow told Suzanne that night, do that to me again.

"Why don't you come down to watch crew anymore?" Blair asked Sparrow as they sat on the wall in front of the school watching for Suzanne.

Sparrow shrugged. "Its dumb."

"We're locked up all day in a school full of girls and you think it's dumb to go and gaze at half-naked men? You're losing it, Sparrow. Really."

Blair pulled on her hair. She had explained earlier that pulling it made it stick out more. She had shaved half of it off and dyed tendrils on the other half a robin's-egg blue.

5

"Where is she anyway?" Blair said.

"Detained," Sparrow said sarcastically.

"Maybe I should call my father."

"She'll be here. Eventually."

"I can't wait to get my license. Then I can drive myself down here. I want to go to 33 Dunster Street and use my fake ID to order tequila sunrises."

"That's dumb," Sparrow said.

"Why?"

"It just is."

"You are so straight. Honestly. You'd probably order pink ladies."

Why is she always late? Sparrow thought.

"I don't think it would kill Jessica to have us wait at her house," Blair said. "It's right down the street. She's got the new Dead Kennedys album. We could at least be listening to it while we wait."

"Here she is," Sparrow said, relieved.

"Am I late?" Suzanne said as they climbed into the backseat. "I rushed like mad."

"You're always late when you pick us up," Sparrow said. "Blair's father is punctual one hundred percent of the time."

"He's a painter. He works at home. So he has more flexibility," Suzanne said.

"She's never late for Ron," Sparrow said to Blair.

"How was practice?" Suzanne asked.

Sparrow leaned over the front seat. "Can we stop at Brigham's?"

Her mother looked at her watch. This was an image etched forever in Sparrow's mind—her mother glancing at her watch and sighing. When Sparrow was younger, she used to feel bad for her mother. She thought she worked too hard. At night sometimes, Sparrow would make the baby-sitter leave food out for her—cookies and milk, pea-

6

nut butter and jelly sandwiches, graham crackers. Lately, though, her mother's ambition and efficiency disturbed Sparrow. She wanted them to spend more time together. It seemed as if all of Suzanne's spare time went to Ron. How could her mother have Ron intrude on their life when she'd never even let Sparrow's real father in?

"I guess we have time for some ice cream," Suzanne said.

Brigham's smelled like spilled milk. The bright lights there made everyone look paler, colors faded against the glaring whiteness. They slid into a booth, the red vinyl crackling beneath them.

"I think you have something in your hair," Suzanne said, reaching across the booth and touching Blair's head.

"It's dyed, Mom," Sparrow said.

"No. There's something blue. Like paint."

"It's a hair coloring," Blair said. "Like a hair spray."

Suzanne frowned. "Oh."

"Her father thinks it looks swell," Sparrow said.

"He gave me this," Blair said. She lifted up the silver peace sign that hung on a chain around her neck for Suzanne to see. "You must have one of these somewhere, don't you? My father's got so much neat stuff. He's got a motorcycle jacket with an American flag on the back like the one in *Easy Rider* and this really neat poster that has a flower drawn on it and underneath it says 'War is bad for flowers and other living things.' "

"My mother throws everything away," she said. "She doesn't think it's healthy to dwell on the past."

Suzanne sipped her coffee. Sometimes, like right now, she got a certain pained look on her face that made her look young and vulnerable. It made Sparrow want to go over to her and hug her. Instead, Sparrow pushed at her sundae, mixing the ice cream into the hot fudge.

ANN HOOD

"My father even got arrested for protesting the war," Blair said proudly. "Twice."

"Arrested?" Sparrow said. "He has a criminal record?"

"They used to just put them in jail overnight," Suzanne said. "It happened to some friends of mine back in college."

Tell me, Sparrow thought. Please.

Suzanne motioned for the check.

"Look at the time," she said with a sigh. "I've got to meet Ron at the Hampshire House in an hour."

Sparrow tried to catch her mother's eye. The softness had left her face again. She looked older, in control. The spell was broken.

Sparrow thought that her father still lived in Maine. That was where her parents had met in college. She had a vague memory of going there once to see him. She could imagine a huge Christmas tree with tiny white lights. Sparrow's mother said that yes, they had visited there once and that there may have been such a tree. She really couldn't recall the details.

Sparrow had lived most of her life with her mother in the same large apartment in Boston overlooking Logan Airport, Boston Harbor, and the south roof of Quincy Market. To Sparrow, the building looked like a hospital. She hated it. Sometimes, she dreamed of living in the woods with her father in Maine.

December.

"Susan," her mother said, "there's some fruit and Brie in the kitchen if you get hungry." She was wearing her black silk dress and large square clip-on rhinestone earrings. "We should be in early."

Sparrow kept reading. Her mother had eaten out with Ron every night that week.

8

"Susan, did you hear me?"

Sparrow did not look up.

"I'll tell you what. Tomorrow night I'll invite Ron to dinner here. We'll have take-out Chinese. That's your favorite, right?"

Sparrow shrugged.

"He is really very special to me," her mother said. She sat on the couch beside Sparrow.

Sparrow closed her book and focused on the lights of a plane landing at the airport across the harbor.

"Who knows," her mother said, "maybe this will turn into something more permanent."

The plane was circling.

"If I had to make a list of the traits the man of my dreams would have," Suzanne continued, "Ron would have them all. I used to do things like that when I was your age. Make lists of the perfect men, the perfect wedding." Suzanne laughed. "He's smart, thoughtful, ambitious—"

"He sounds like a boy scout," Sparrow said.

"—not to mention, adorable."

Sparrow rolled her eyes.

"Well, I think he is," Suzanne said. "And he's so easy to be with. Remember when he took us to see *42nd Street*? And for seafood at Anthony's?"

Sparrow looked at her mother. "The play was stupid. Innocuous," she said carefully.

Her mother smiled. "Innocuous. Yes, I suppose it was. But the night was fun. I mean, the three of us together like that."

"I would never describe Ron as fun."

"That's not fair, Susan. He's very nice to you. You haven't given him a chance. And he's so fond of you."

Her mother rose, went to the bar, and poured a Chivas on the rocks.

"We have talked about it," she said after she took a sip.

"What?"

"Ron and I have discussed the possibility of marriage."

"Oh." Sparrow squirmed uncomfortably. Another plane was getting ready to land now. She watched the red flashing lights on the wings.

"It looks like we might do it. Merge, as Ron says." Her mother smiled, also uncomfortable.

Sparrow kept her eyes focused on the plane. She wondered briefly if it was coming from Maine.

"How do you feel about that?"

Sparrow shrugged.

"I know that it may take some time for you to get used to the idea. I mean, having a man around the house after all this time will certainly be strange. For me too. Shaving cream and boxer shorts everywhere." Her mother laughed. "And men are such strange creatures. Your father used to—"

Sparrow's head jerked around to face her mother.

Her mother inhaled quickly, then took another drink of her scotch.

"What?" Sparrow asked.

"I don't know what possessed me to bring that up."

Sparrow continued to look at her mother, waiting for more. Her mother drank again, averted her eyes.

"He used to have this routine at night. He would take a drink of water, then fluff up his pillow, stretch, fluff up his pillow again, and then get into bed. Odd of me to think of that. It's just, well, men are such strange creatures." Her mother's eye met Sparrow's again. "I've noticed that Ron puts salt on his food before he even tastes it. If that isn't the strangest thing."

The intercom buzzed.

"He's here," Suzanne said. "You know, he wants

you to like him. It was really important to him that I talk to you about all of this. I mean, he's concerned about how you feel about it." She touched Sparrow's arm lightly. "I want you to like him too. He's the kind of man I'd like for you someday."

No thank you, Sparrow thought.

The intercom buzzed again.

"Tomorrow night will be your night," her mother said. "We'll get take-out or go into Chinatown. Whichever you prefer. The three of us. How does that sound?"

"Boring," Sparrow said as her mother went to the door. "It sounds boring."

Suzanne came back holding on to Ron's arm. She looked girlish. In her free hand she held a long-stemmed white rose. Ron was short with horn-rimmed glasses. When he smiled, he looked unnatural, like someone from a horror movie who had been zapped by aliens. When he entered a room, the smell of Paco Rabanne was so strong that Sparrow was forced to gag slightly. Ron was nothing like the sexy men in the cologne's ad, who pounded at typewriters in rundown beach houses or called their lovers from rumpled brass beds. Instead, Ron looked like a corporate executive, which, in fact, he was. He always sat very straight and never loosened his tie, even in extreme heat or after a long day. When he and Sparrow's mother were together, they never touched. They walked briskly in perfect step.

"Hello, Susan," Ron said. "I brought this for you." He handed Sparrow a thin volume of poetry. "Your mother tells me you admire Frost."

"I like Allen Ginsberg or Gregory Corso, actually."

"Ginsberg?" Ron looked questioningly at Sparrow's mother. "I thought—"

"She's just being ornery again."

Ron smiled. "Ah!"

11

"We'll be at Maison Robert," her mother said. "There's Brie and fruit in the kitchen. And smoked turkey, too, I think."

"Mother was just telling me," Sparrow said, "that my father used to have this funny routine that he would do every night. Before they went to bed."

Ron and her mother exchanged glances.

"We were discussing the changes that would occur if there were a man around the house," her mother said.

"Ah," Ron said again.

"Yes," Sparrow said as she opened her book again. "It would be awful."

"Susan!" her mother said.

"Just for the record, Ron, my name is not Susan. It's Sparrow. I'm sure my father calls me Sparrow."

"Well, then," Ron said. "Sparrow it is."

REBEKAH, 1985

The worst insult in the entire school was to accuse someone of liking Rebekah Morgan. Sally Perkins, head cheerleader since junior high, had just shouted the insult to her old boyfriend. She enjoyed breaking his heart. And tormenting him. So, after she told him she was going to the Freshman Frolic with someone else, she added with a toss of her blond ponytail: "Anyway, I heard you like Rebekah Morgan." All the boys groaned and pretended to throw up. Rebekah froze. She stood against her locker, clutching her books, and prayed she would disappear. "Hi, Becky," Sally said sweetly as she walked by with her friends. "Rebekah Morgan," the boy groaned as he fell to the floor. "Ugh!"

Rebekah's entire life was a series of such humiliations. She had an early memory of her family walking through town on a hot July afternoon and people pointing and whispering "look at those hippies." All of her life, Rebekah hated the large sprawling house that they lived in and the pottery workshop and store behind it. She

13

longed to eat Twinkies with her lunch instead of dried fruit and nuts. She wished her family had a Ford station wagon. But when she told her mother her wish, Elizabeth said, "Legs don't make pollution." Why, Rebekah wondered as she worked at the pottery store every weekend, couldn't she have a job scooping ice cream at Friendly's, and a pink and white bedroom in a split-level house? "Methinks," her father said when she complained to him, "thou doth protest too much." Lately, Rebekah was very aware that he was going bald.

Rebekah had decided that the source of her humiliation was her nose. Despite her mother's donation of carob brownies to the junior high bake sale and her father's refusal to pay income tax and the organic garden in their yard—despite everything—Rebekah decided that it was indeed her nose that placed her in the caste of Untouchable at school. Her nose was large and sprawling, like her house. And it had a bump on it. If it were small and smooth, Rebekah thought, life would be all right.

It was mid-summer and the kitchen smelled like damson plums. The sweet smell hung in the air. Rebekah was boiling jars for the jam while her mother stirred the plums in a large pot on the stove. Outside, her father, Howard, and her brother, Jesse, tossed a Frisbee. The sun bounced off the copper countertops in the kitchen, caught in the grooves and scratches acquired from hundreds of loaves of bread being kneaded there and pounds of vegetables being chopped.

Her mother hummed, "Ode to Joy" it sounded like, and Rebekah was suddenly struck with guilt at her secret longings to be somebody else, to look different and have a different family. This was, after all, *her* family. Last spring they had bicycled to Canada, the four of them. Their faces and arms and legs had browned from the sun. Her father had made her a necklace from tiny shells they found on a beach. On their first night in Canada, they had stayed at a fancy hotel and eaten a banquet of fresh fish in a restaurant that overlooked the ocean. Rebekah's mother took pictures of the trip and when they got home Rebekah helped her develop them. They worked together in the upstairs bathroom, her mother explaining exactly what to do.

Now Rebekah studied her mother's face. Her hair, like Rebekah's, was black and unruly. She had it tied in a braid. Wiry strands had found their way free and stuck out around her head. Some of them were gray.

"Mom," Rebekah said.

Elizabeth stopped humming and looked at Rebekah. They both had large dark eyes. Rebekah looked into a face that would look just like her own in twenty years—unless she did something. In the middle of that face was the same large nose, dominating the eyes, towering over the mouth.

"I have a problem," Rebekah said. "A big problem."

Her mother nodded.

"When was the last time I had a friend here?"

"What's the point, Rebekah?"

"The point . . . is, the problem—"

"What is it?"

"My nose."

"Your nose? Does it hurt? Bleed? Run?" Elizabeth leaned toward her, inspected her nose, touched it, prodded it gently.

"No," Rebekah said, and pulled away. "It just *is*. It's huge and bumpy and it's ruining my life."

"Rebekah, how is your life ruined?"

15

"No one will talk to me at school. Everyone laughs at me. With this nose, who can blame them? The only boy who has ever even noticed me is Henry and he's weird. I'm ugly." This last she added in a whisper. It was too awful and too true to say out loud.

"Bekah, you're not ugly. You're beautiful—"

"Don't tell me I'm beautiful—"

And together they said: "—inside, where it matters."

"All right. That's not what you need to hear."

"I've got to get a new one."

"A new one?"

"Lots of people get them."

"Wait a minute—"

"Mom, I can't wait. My life is a disaster." And then she began the argument for the idea that she had practiced in her mind. "I need a nose job. I need it more than food or clothes or anything in the world. It's the only solution."

Elizabeth sighed and wiped her forehead. "Your nose is just like my nose. People like me, don't they? I had friends and dates and you will too. Soon enough."

"Soon enough? I'm already fifteen, Mom. When is it going to happen? When I'm thirty and gray and even uglier?"

"If people are judging you because of your nose, then they are not the type of people you want as friends. You said yourself that Henry likes you. Nose and all." Her mother waited for her to smile and agree but she didn't. Instead, Rebekah just stared at her, her face wrinkled in an attempt to stop the tears from falling. Elizabeth shook her head. "Your nose is not ruining your life. And I think you know that."

Rebekah looked away from her mother and out the window. Her father and Jesse were sitting on the grass.

She watched her father. He was talking and moving his hands around and around, explaining, it seemed, about making pottery. He had studied in Japan to be a potter. Every time he lit the kiln, he gave an offering of sake to insure a good fire. Her parents had dedicated most of their lives to their beliefs, to living as pure and natural a life as they could. And now these beliefs were dooming her to a life of misery, a life with a huge nose. Rebekah imagined the years ahead of her, her nose growing larger as she grew older. She would be forced to live here forever and make pottery. The thought made her shudder. There must be a way, she thought.

Rebekah watched as her father worked with the clay, spinning, shaping, smoothing.

"Dad," she said, "what do you think of Mom's nose?"

Her father laughed. "I think it looks like her mother's nose."

"And mine."

He glanced at her. "Yes. And like yours."

"It's a pretty big nose," Rebekah said.

"It's not so big. Look at Karl Malden. Or Jimmy Durante."

"They're men. Old men."

"Barbra Streisand."

Rebekah sighed. It was useless.

"What's all this about?" Howard said.

"I'm thinking about getting cosmetic surgery."

"Really?" he asked, amused.

"This isn't funny, Daddy. My life is ruined. By this." She pointed to her nose.

"Oh, Bekah," he said, "you don't have such a bad life. School will start again soon and everything will be fine. Summer has a way of making us bored. Lethargic. Come here, work on this vase awhile. Can you see the shape I'm trying to achieve here?"

Rebekah looked over. To her, the bumpy and mis-shapen clay looked exactly like her nose.

School was beginning in six weeks. Rebekah circled the day in red on her calendar. She sat on the bed and stared at the circled day looming before her. She would not, she vowed, go to school with this nose. Instead, she would walk into her homeroom with a tiny, turned-up nose. Boys would gape, girls would stare, and her life would change. She might even try out for cheerleader.

Rebekah opened the Yellow Pages to Surgeons, Plastic and her finger settled randomly on one. Charles Warren, M.D. Charles Warren, M.D., would understand the importance of a smaller nose, she thought. He had grown up, no doubt, and still resided in, a world of perfect profiles. No bumps. No flaring nostrils. He would look at her nose and understand.

"Fifteen hundred dollars," Charles Warren, M.D., said.

Rebekah gasped. One thousand five hundred dollars.

"And a parent or guardian must sign the consent form. Unless you're eighteen. You're not eighteen, are you?"

Rebekah shook her head. She looked into the pink face of Dr. Warren. His hair was blond and he wore rimless glasses. He looked like he belonged to a country club. His nose was perfect.

"You won't look like Brooke Shields," he said. "Everyone these days wants to look like Brooke Shields."

Rebekah assured him she did not.

"That's what they all say." He lifted her face toward

the light. "You will look better. A definite improvement."

That was enough for Rebekah. Better. An improvement.

"May I have a consent form, please?"

Every Saturday Rebekah worked in the pottery store.
In summer, tourists en route to Tanglewood or to the
Norman Rockwell Museum found their way to her parents' store. Middle-aged women with stiff blond hair bought
wedding presents for their nieces. Younger women in
Polo shirts and wraparound skirts bought entire sets of
dishes. "No one will have anything like this," they would
say as they cooed over the different patterns. Rebekah
hated working there. She hated smiling at these people
and explaining how her father had learned the art in
Japan.

Today was no different. The store was hot and dusty,
filled with people in brightly colored summer clothes.

"Can I put these in a dishwasher?" a tanned woman
wearing monogrammed glasses asked.

"Yes," Rebekah said for the tenth time that day.

The line of customers at the register was long. Rebekah
took the money mechanically. Hurricane lamps, coffee
mugs, vases. She made change, wrapped the pieces.

"Can you change a hundred?" a man asked. "I only
have a hundred." He was holding a baby. The baby had
on a T-shirt that said DAVE'S DAUGHTER.

"Sure," Rebekah said.

She took the hundred-dollar bill and began to make
change. Suddenly, her hands froze. Her eyes darted down
to the cash drawer. There were fifties, twenties, tens—
stacks of them. This was the third hundred-dollar bill she
had changed that day. There was, in the drawer, much
more than $1500. There was probably twice that. She

fingered the money she was holding and smiled. Here, before her, was her new nose.

There were no secrets in Rebekah's family. Her parents smoked marijuana in front of her. She had seen her father naked. And she knew that they kept all their money in a strongbox in their bedroom closet. Today, Rebekah watched as her father collected the money from the till. He was tall and muscular, with shiny blue eyes. With his friendly face and deep laugh, he reminded Rebekah of Santa Claus. Until recently, she used to love to climb into his lap and bury her face and fingers in his beard.

"Want to run away to South America?" he asked her, laughing as he put the money into an envelope.

Guilt hit Rebekah so hard she doubled over slightly.

Howard's smile disappeared. "You okay?"

"Yes," she said as she straightened. "Yes."

While her parents and Jesse were out for a walk, Rebekah opened the strongbox. She slowly counted out fifteen hundred dollars. It didn't seem to leave even a tiny dent in the pile of money in the box. She put the money on the bureau and smoothed out the wrinkles. It seemed like so little, really. Rebekah saw before her an autumn day when she would walk into school with her new nose. She would wear her hair loose that day, and put on blush and lip gloss. She would have on a plaid skirt, Izod shirt, and loafers with tassles. Rebekah bit her bottom lip. She knew that taking the money was wrong. It was, in fact, a crime. Maybe even grand larceny. But she also knew that without it, her life was over. As one hand clutched the money, the other traced the bridge of her nose, paused over the bump.

She heard the screen door slam downstairs and the

sound of voices. Her father laughed. Rebekah folded the fifteen hundred dollars and shoved it deep into the pocket of her jeans. She could always put the money back, she thought. For now, just having it there, seemed enough. She closed the strongbox and put it back into the closet.

Lined up against the wall in Rebekah's room were more than a dozen large teddy bears in fancy costumes. Henry and his brother had surprised her and delivered them one day. Secretly, Rebekah loved them, thought they were funny and chic. But Henry was, like her nose, a constant reminder of her oddness. Before her parents went into the pottery business, they had lived on and run a produce farm with Henry's parents. To Rebekah, being the daughter of a potter was only slightly better than being the child of a farmer. The farm was no longer a working one, and Henry's father sold copy machines in Western Massachusetts and Vermont. If it weren't for all these things, Henry might seem a little more interesting. But all those things were there.

Howard and Elizabeth were having a clambake. They invited fifty people. There were kegs of beer and jugs of wine and the air was rich with the salty smell of clams and fish and lobster. Rebekah's father had strung twinkling Christmas lights in all the trees, and as darkness approached, the yard was illuminated by tiny flashes of pink and green and blue and white. Someone had brought sparklers. Henry handed her a lit one, shooting and hissing. Rebekah accepted it silently.

"Want to get high?" he asked, settling cross-legged beside her.

Rebekah shook her head.

Henry shrugged and watched his sparkler dance about.

Rebekah watched hers as well. The day after tomorrow she would have her new nose. She had seen Dr. Warren again, forged the consent form, had two photos taken (profile and full face), given blood and urine specimens. Dr. Warren had assured her the bruises would be gone by the time school started.

"I'm going away to school," Henry said. "To Brown."

Rebekah nodded.

"Yeah. I leave in a few weeks."

Rebekah's sparkler died and she dropped it to the ground.

"I can't keep those bears, Henry. They're expensive."

"I don't want them back," he said. "They're for you."

Rebekah looked at him. He had liked her since they were small children and both of their families lived together on the farm. As far as Rebekah could tell, Henry was the only boy who ever liked her. And Henry's family was even odder than her own. His mother had stopped sending him to school when he was twelve because she was worried he would be kidnapped or killed. A reporter from the *Boston Globe* heard the story and did a human interest feature on the family in their Sunday magazine. With the article there had been a slightly out of focus picture of Henry's entire weird family. His mother, Claudia, who stopped cutting her hair and fingernails "to see how long they'll grow, like when you die," kept referring to Henry as Simon, Henry's dead brother. Rebekah could not have Henry, of all people, like her.

"Could you get me some wine?" Rebekah asked him.

She watched him lope away. He was tall, too tall, with extra-long legs and arms. His hair was the palest blond, almost white, and thin on top, which made his forehead too large and prominent. Rebekah decided he looked a little like an ape. He returned with two plastic glasses and a jug full of red wine.

As he poured them each a glass full, he smiled. There was no denying that despite everything else, Henry had a very nice smile.

"To us," he said, and he lifted his glass to hers.

Rebekah drank the wine quickly and refilled her glass.

"It tastes good," she said to Henry. Good-bye old nose, she thought as she drained the second glass.

A group of people started to dance the twist. Rebekah caught a glimpse of her parents. Elizabeth was wearing a green and blue striped skirt that puffed out slightly as she danced. Howard laughed, mocked embarrassment at the sight of his wife's knees when her skirt lifted. Rebekah had taken money from these people, her parents. Grand larceny, she thought.

Henry said something, but "Twist And Shout" was too loud for Rebekah to understand him. She didn't want to hear him anyway. She watched her parents dance. They twisted down to the ground, then worked their way back up. Rebekah remembered her mother teaching her to twist. She had taken a bath towel and held it behind her. "It's like drying up after a bath," Elizabeth had said, and they twisted together in the hallway, their partners fluffy striped towels. Rebekah closed her eyes. She was dizzy from the wine. She was forgetting the importance of her new nose, she reminded herself. And once her life had improved, her parents would see its importance too. Quickly, Rebekah finished her wine and poured some more. She was only two days away from her new life.

Henry was talking again.

"What?" Rebekah said.

He leaned closer to her. "It's so noisy. Can we go somewhere to talk?"

23

Rebekah's mother waved over at them, smiled.

"Yes," Rebekah said, "let's go somewhere."

She took Henry into the pottery workshop. They drank more wine and smoked a joint. Rebekah explained about the kiln and the sake offerings.

"Neat," Henry said as he peeked into the kiln.

Rebekah asked Henry about Brown. As he talked, she remembered that Sally Perkins, Head Cheerleader and Most Popular Girl, used to have a boyfriend at Brown. She had worn his fraternity pin and all the girls had crowded around her to see it. Rebekah studied Henry more closely. She had to narrow her eyes to focus. If she were to arrive at school with a new nose and a boyfriend at Brown, her place in the senior class would be secured. Henry, she decided after careful scrutiny, was not so bad after all. He did not have acne or any bad scars. And, she noted, besides his nice smile, he had a very nice nose.

Henry stopped talking.

"Your glass is empty," Rebekah said, and refilled it for him. She had a rather pleasant feeling, like she was floating. In fact, she felt like she was swooping around like an eagle—she swooped her arms to pick up the wine and then swooped toward her glass. She leaned over and Henry's face flew by her. Rebekah giggled.

"You know," she said, and was surprised at how far away her own voice sounded, "this is a going-away party."

"For me?" Henry asked. His voice echoed slightly in her ears.

"No. Well, yes, that too, I suppose. But for this, I mean." She pointed to her nose. "Here. Feel." She took Henry's hand and ran it slowly over the bump. Henry's touch felt surprisingly nice. "Oh," she said.

Henry's face appeared suddenly in front of her own. He kissed her, a soft little kiss which felt very good.

24

My first kiss, Rebekah thought. She didn't want him to stop.

Henry gently kissed her nose.

"Yes," she said solemnly, "kiss it good-bye."

He pulled away from her. The motion made her dizzy and she had to grab his arm to steady herself.

"What are you talking about?" he said.

"I'm getting it fixed." Then she added sadly, "It's so ugly."

"But you're so beautiful."

"Maybe on the inside. But no one ever looks there."

"I do," he whispered, and kissed her some more.

They kissed for a very long time, it seemed. Rebekah still heard The Lovin' Spoonful in the distance. She tried to block out the image of her parents dancing out there and to concentrate instead on Henry. He was breathing heavily, and pressing against her. He thinks I'm beautiful, Rebekah thought. It felt so good, to be kissing him and listening to him breathe this way. But then Rebekah felt the chalky dust fill her nose and throat.

She rose unsteadily, her stomach rolling unevenly.

"I think I will keep the bears," she said.

Henry pushed her gently down to the dusty floor. Rebekah was amazed at how long kissing could go on. For a minute, she saw the kissing here, in the pottery workshop, as a kind of communion. It was this dust, after all, that was buying her new nose. Maybe, she thought, this is more like a burial. But before she could think about it anymore, she felt as if a magnet pulled at her, pulled her around and around. She tried to get her eyes to focus, but everything was spinning too quickly. Images of Henry and the kiln sped by so fast that before she could register, they were gone, only to return a second later at an even faster speed.

"Rebekah?" Henry said.

She gagged, the taste of pottery dust and wine in her throat.

Henry moved quickly, got her outside, held her head while she was sick.

"It's okay," he said over and over.

He stroked her hair and then her cheeks and finally, with one thin finger, her nose.

"It's okay," he said again.

But the smell of the pottery workshop stayed in her and she had to turn her head away, gasping for air.

Rebekah looked into the coffee cup in front of her, the mirror image of her mother sitting across from her. Rebekah was sore all over. And her head ached. She could not believe, as she sat here in the bright kitchen with her family, that last night she had kissed Henry. Henry of all people. She would never, she vowed, talk to him again. She would never drink wine again.

"Rebekah kissed Henry," Jesse said.

Rebekah's head shot up, sending the throbbing pain from her temples throughout her head.

"I saw you," he said.

Elizabeth looked up. "Interesting."

"I did not," Rebekah said.

"I *saw* you."

"He has always liked you," Elizabeth said.

Rebekah rubbed her aching head.

"In the pottery workshop," Jesse added.

"Is that where you disappeared to?"

"Please, Mom," Rebekah said wearily.

"He's leaving for college, isn't he?"

"Brown." I wish, she added to herself, he was already gone.

It was over. Rebekah's head and face pounded from the pain. She had two black eyes and bandages that extended over her nose and cheeks. She was in her bedroom with an ice pack on her forehead. Her parents and Jesse had gone to Tanglewood to hear a concert. They would come home and find her face a bruised and swollen mess. And they would be furious. The longest she could delay the confrontation was until the next morning. She prayed she would die peacefully during the night.

A knock on her bedroom door woke Rebekah with a start.

"Henry's on the phone," her mother said through the door.

Rebekah realized that she was indeed still alive, her prayers unanswered. The sunlight hurt her eyes. Rebekah groaned. Her face hurt and Henry was on the phone. She forced herself to think of that September day that would make all this worthwhile.

"I'll tell him you're sleeping."

Rebekah listened to her mother's footsteps fade. She could not leave this room. She could not face her mother.

"Rebekah, he'll call this afternoon."

"Mom, could you—"

The doorknob began to turn.

"Don't come in!" Rebekah shrieked.

"Why ever not?" The door remained frozen, slightly opened.

"Please send Dad in."

"Rebekah, he's working. What's going on?"

Tears began to fall down Rebekah's swollen face. The throbbing behind her eyes and cheekbones got worse as she cried.

"I need to see Daddy."

"For goodness' sake." Elizabeth closed the door and once again Rebekah listened to her walk away.

It took a long time for her father to come from the workshop. Rebekah heard her mother call to him. She knew that she had a lot of explaining to do and Rebekah wanted to do it to her father's kind Santa Claus face. She could picture her mother if she told her. Her lips would tighten, her jaw would twitch.

Rebekah remembered the time she had bought steak for Jesse and herself. Her parents had gone to Boston for the day and left Rebekah money to buy something for dinner. The steaks had caught her eye, sparkling red in the meat section, an area she was usually rushed through by her mother. "We are not cannibals," Elizabeth would say. Rebekah had bought the steaks. She and Jesse had stared at the cooked meat on their plates, watching as the blood slowly oozed out of it and formed watery red puddles around the steak. "What's the matter?" Rebekah had said angrily as Jesse stared, horrified. "Haven't you ever eaten a steak before?" And she cut into hers and placed a piece into her mouth. She was completely unprepared for the slipperiness of it, or the toughness when she chewed it. But she and Jesse ate every bite. When their parents got home, both children had stomachaches. "Rebekah made me eat cow," Jesse cried. Elizabeth's lips tightened and her jaw twitched. "Well," Howard said, "there's nothing wrong with trying something different." And he had given Rebekah a big wink.

"Can I come in?" her father asked now.

"Yes. But be prepared."

"Your mother thinks you cut your hair while we were out yesterday," he laughed as he walked in. His smile disappeared when he saw her.

"Were you attacked, Bekah?" he asked, his eyes so filled with concern that she began to sob again.

28

"No."

Howard frowned. "What then?"

"I had it done."

"What?"

"My nose!"

Her father took her into his arms.

"I was ugly. So ugly. No one would even be my friend." The words escaped in gasps between the sobbing. "I tried to ask you for help. And Mom too. But no one listened. So I just went and did it. Myself."

Rebekah buried her pained face in her father's beard, and burrowed her fingers into it as she cried.

The family sat around the dining room table, a massive block of oak with six legs. In the center was a vase the color of wet dirt, filled with yellow daisies. The question they were considering was about Rebekah. She had sat in her room for three weeks, coming out only to eat and work in the pottery store, which she did every day from ten to six in order to pay back the fifteen hundred dollars. Her nose was still slightly swollen and the remaining bruises were the color of Dijon mustard. Her mother could not look at her without her jaw twitching. The punishment was indefinite. It stretched before Rebekah like an endless tunnel. In her exile she started and finished *The Clan of the Cave Bear*. Yesterday she began *The Valley of Horses*.

They were here at the table to decide if Rebekah should be allowed to accompany them to the Wickford Art Show. The family went every year, setting up a table along the streets of the small seaside town in Rhode Island. They sold pottery and handed out brochures about the technique Howard used. On the way home after the last night, they always ate Chinese food at a restaurant called Pagoda Inn. It was a family ritual.

Every time Rebekah looked up, Jesse made his eyes go crossed. Only in this family, Rebekah thought, would a ten-year-old get a say in the decision-making process. He had acquired a silver space suit, someone's discarded Halloween costume, and wore it constantly.

"You just don't seem to appreciate the seriousness of what you did," Elizabeth said.

"The prisoner shows no remorse," Rebekah said.

Elizabeth's jaw twitched.

They glared at each other across the daisies.

"I would like everyone to go to the art show. I would like us to be there as a family. All of us," Howard said.

"Let's vote, please," Rebekah pleaded.

"It's not only the art show at issue here, Rebekah," Elizabeth said. "There's no point in punishment if it's not making you think about what you did."

"I've already told you that I thought about it for weeks before I did it. It will all be worth it. You'll see."

Her parents exchanged glances.

"Look," Rebekah said, "I don't want to spoil anything. I'll do whatever you want so we can all go. One big happy family."

"Well," Howard said, "let's see what happens in another month of you working in the shop and staying home. Elizabeth?"

Her mother nodded.

Rebekah sighed. Freedom was another month away. It looked as if she would finish *The Valley of Horses* too.

The bruises, though not completely gone, were easily hidden with an Erase-It stick. She did not look like Brooke Shields, but the bump in Rebekah's nose had disappeared. She still had a rather large, ordinary nose.

Rebekah's plans to buy new clothes and makeup did

30

not work out. Instead, all the money she earned at the pottery shop had to go toward paying back her parents. She had to search drawers, closets, and old trunks to find things to wear for the first day of school. Finally, with Vaseline on her lips, an old pleated skirt from the attic, and a short-sleeved cotton sweater of her mother's, she was ready. There were no loafers with tassles or Izod shirt, but with her new nose and high spirits, Rebekah thought she looked pretty good.

Downstairs, in the kitchen, the radio played jazz. Her mother was drinking coffee and working on a cross-word puzzle. She looked pale and thinner than usual. Rebekah felt as if she hadn't noticed her mother at all these past few weeks. She poured a glass of orange juice and looked out the window. It was a perfect day. She had sacrificed everything for this day, and it was here at last. Tucked into her book bag was a card from Henry, slipped to her during her exile. At lunch today, with Sally Perkins within hearing distance, she would casually pull it out and read it. "My boyfriend at Brown," she would explain.

"It's about that time, isn't it?" Elizabeth asked. "Daddy filled your tires. They were low."

"I'm walking. No one rides bikes."

"Then you'd really better get going."

Rebekah turned from the window, smiled at her mother. It was too good a day to let their animosity get in the way.

"What do you have on your lips?"

"Just Vaseline."

"Well, they won't get chapped anyway."

"Very funny."

"Bekah?"

"What?"

"I don't want you to be disappointed today."

31

"Disappointed?"

"I don't know what you're expecting—"

"Nothing. I'm not expecting anything. God! You want to ruin everything for me, don't you?"

"Okay. I'm sorry. I just don't want you to get hurt."

Rebekah gathered her things.

"Have a good day," she heard her mother say as she left.

Rebekah sat under a tree in the front yard. The humiliation was so horrible she couldn't even move. In fact, she was not sure how she made it home. This day, her new start, the beginning of her life filled with parties and dates and giggling girlfriends, had been a failure. She sacrificed everything for this day and it was all for nothing.

Tears filled her eyes, rolled down her still-tender cheeks and nose. It was over. Tomorrow she would don her patched jeans and bicycle to school like before. It didn't matter. Her nose was different, but everything else was still the same. She had no car to borrow from her parents so she could drive to McDonald's and sit on the hood while she sipped Coke and ate a Big Mac. She didn't even eat hamburgers.

Rebekah stretched out under the tree, looked up at the clear blue sky. Rebekah Morgan got a nose job, everyone had whispered. At lockers and in gym class and in notes hastily scribbled during English. Rebekah Morgan got a nose job. Rebekah knew she must go inside and tell her parents she was wrong, that it had all been a big mistake. She must continue to work at the pottery store to repay the rest of the money. She must write to Henry and apologize for misleading him. She would probably even return all the bears. Her hand traced her nose, lingered on the spot where the bump used to be. There was so much she had to do. But first, she had to just lie there, under the oak tree, and cry.

HOWARD AND ELIZABETH, 1985

All that Howard could think of was the water bed they had when they first moved into their house. Elizabeth had never liked it. She used to say that if she wanted to sleep on water, she'd take a trip on the *Queen Mary*. But he had loved that bed. It was like being lulled to sleep each night. He liked the way he could feel Elizabeth beside him, her movements registering with tiny sloshes. Now, on this sturdy mattress, in the dark, he couldn't tell if she was even beside him at all.

Then her voice came through the darkness.

"Let's talk about the farm," Elizabeth said.

Oh, God, Howard thought. This is bad. What is happening here is so bad.

But he said, "All right."

He heard her sigh.

"Should I put on a light?" he said.

He heard a match strike, and watched in its glow as Elizabeth lit a candle beside the bed.

"You know," she said, the candle sending a small shadow across her face, "all the time you were in Vietnam and Rebekah and I were in New York, I kept getting these letters from Claudia about how beautiful the Berkshires were. I remember in one of them she described going to an outdoor concert, at Tanglewood, with Simon. She described the smells and the way the hills looked and how beautiful the music sounded, clean and pure, she said. They ate freshly picked strawberries and blueberries. I read that letter and looked out our window onto Broome Street with all the trucks and noise and soot and I thought how nice a farm would be."

Howard thought back to when Jesse was a baby. One night, his temperature was so high that he went into convulsions. They sat in the hospital waiting room while the doctors packed him in ice to bring the fever down. Sitting there, they never talked about Jesse being so sick, or what would they do if something happened to him. Instead, they talked about the farm.

Howard felt Elizabeth waiting for him to say something.

"When you showed me those letters from Claudia," he said, "I could still smell the jungle on my skin. The idea of starting over in the country was like an answered prayer."

Elizabeth's hand reached for his under the covers. He traced the fingers, the palm. Sometimes, he thought, prayers are answered. Jesse had been all right that terrible night they rushed him to the hospital.

"When you were gone," Elizabeth was saying, "I remember getting some paintings ready for my show at the gallery and I was furious at you for not being with me. I thought, I've got this cranky kid and paintings to finish and bills to pay. How dare he not be here? How dare he be so far away?"

"But," he said, "we would never have bought the farm if I hadn't gone to Vietnam. I would have stayed at Columbia until we turned into the perfect academic couple. Of course, you could have played with your painting as a side thing."

She laughed. "I make terrible martinis. Our cocktail parties for the dean and professors would have been terrible flops."

"And your canapes aren't so great either."

"You know, whenever I think of New York, it's never of me alone there with Rebekah while you were in Vietnam. It's always of the time when all three of us were there. The other time seems like a dream. How did we get through it?"

"I was so afraid to die," he said without thinking.

Their eyes met briefly.

"Let's talk about the farm," she said.

"Yes." He put his arms around her tightly. "I'll never forget the first time we saw it. Claudia and Peter were standing in front when we drove up and their kids were playing with those soft balls—"

"Nerf balls."

"That's right. Nerf balls. I remember that crab-apple tree was full of fruit. It smelled so wonderful."

"Later we made jam from it."

"The farm was just what we were looking for."

"It was. A dream—"

"A dream come true."

There was was a brief silence.

"What was your favorite thing there?" Elizabeth asked at last.

Howard didn't answer right away. Instead, he was flooded with images and smells that he kept tucked away for nights like this one. He let them all surge forward now: the feel of the water on his naked body as he swam in the pond at night; the smell of the air there after a summer rain, like newly laundered clothes; the way the moonlight filled their bedroom with a strangely tree-filtered white light; Elizabeth's body in that light, tiny freckles on her arms and back and the salty taste of her.

He shook his head to clear the images. Howard knew that he must answer, he must keep Elizabeth talking. There were difficult things to discuss. Yet his head felt like one of those plastic bubbles on Rebekah's bureau. A tiny town sat under the dome—a miniature white church and a red house around a pond with a lone skater on it. When the bubble was turned upside down, snow fell. Howard felt like that single skater, out alone on the ice with the bubble turned upside down.

"The pond," he answered finally. "I loved to swim at night there. To take off all my clothes and jump in naked." Once he said this, Howard realized it was probably not the best thing to have chosen. This day, he thought, is too haunted. Too many ghosts.

But Elizabeth smiled. "Yes," she said, "the pond. One time, one of the boys—Henry, I think—got a frog from there and put it in Rebekah's bed while she was sleeping. She's still afraid of frogs to this day."

"Those boys tortured her so."

"Do you know what I liked best?"

Howard shook his head.

"Of course there was so much I loved. Like painting in that loft in the barn. And the pond too. It was wonderful having the pond. But best of all I liked Rebekah's bedroom. When I was a little girl, I wanted a room just like that one. Pale blue walls with puffy white clouds painted on them . . . and a ceiling with silver stars and all the planets. I used to like to pretend I was a bird, you know. I would fly all around, spreading my arms for wings. I wanted a room that would make me feel like I was in the sky flying."

Howard remembered Elizabeth painting those stars and planets on Rebekah's bedroom ceiling.

"I never wanted," she continued, "the basic little-girl pink gingham and white eyelet and gilt-trimmed mirrors."

Howard smiled. Elizabeth would be the little girl who wanted to lie in bed at night and gaze at the stars, who pretended to be a bird and spread her arms to fly.

"Not Rebekah, though," Elizabeth said. "Rebekah wants all the gingham and gilt she can get. She's so much like my mother. My mother always worried about what people would say or think." She sat up now and looked at him. "What will happen to Rebekah?"

"She'll grow up to be beautiful and intelligent. Maybe she won't frown so much then."

"Without me. She'll grow up without me."

The words fell from her mouth like the sharpest arrows, sticking deep into him, forcing him to sit up also.

"Hey," he said when he caught his breath, "I thought we were talking about the farm."

"I'm going to die," she said for the first time out loud.

"The doctor said . . ." They both knew what the doctor had said.

"You can do all the right things," she said, "but it just doesn't matter."

Howard wanted to say something that would make it all better. He wanted to offer her hope or tell her that as long as they were together nothing would happen. The doctor had said it could be a very long time. But they both knew the other half was that it could be a very short time. There are no guarantees, he thought. Simon was seven when he drowned. Still a little boy, really. Or today, Howard thought, today he could walk out of this room and get hit by a falling brick. There were no guarantees. But he didn't say any of this. He just looked up at the ceiling and wished there were silver stars there, and white clouds on the walls around him.

Howard noticed that since they'd been to the doctor in New York, Elizabeth moved slower, more deliberately. She brushed her hair with long, deliberate strokes, spent hours arranging a single vase of flowers. In the two weeks since their visit to Sloan-Kettering, Elizabeth had worked on just one item in the pottery workshop, a teapot. She spent days mixing colors, finally settling on a flat chalky blue and a pink the color of raspberries. She would paint a border, she explained to him, and small splashes of chubby pink flowers.

Today she polished the dining room table. She slowly rubbed linseed oil into its cracks, massaged the wood in firm, swirling motions. Howard was mesmerized by her hands. They were slightly shiny and tinged brown from the oil.

"Would you hang a bird feeder outside the bedroom window?" she asked.

Howard had read an article on death and dying that broke it into seven different steps. He was in the stage of denial. By not thinking about it, it didn't seem real at all. It was as if Elizabeth weren't even sick. Until she said something like that. He knew she was alluding to a time when she would be too sick to go to the bedroom window and look out. A bird feeder would bring the birds right to the window. But he pushed that thought to the back of his mind.

"Sure," he said casually as he concentrated on her hands. Round and round, they rubbed the oil into the table.

Elizabeth had gotten sick very quickly. One day she was fine, talking about a trip to Mexico at Christmastime, and the next day she found lumps under her arms and at the back of her neck. Suddenly their lives were consumed with doctor's visits, blood cell counts, sonograms, and waiting rooms. They had even spent a week in New York visiting a specialist. Every time they had gone for tests or to see the doctor, Howard brought a small pad with him, to sketch ideas for new pieces of pottery, or new patterns. But he could never concentrate on work, and always ended up reading the old *People* magazines that littered the waiting room. He knew more about Joan Collins than he had ever thought possible.

They found a new doctor in Boston that they both liked. He was young, with bright red hair and freckles. His nose was peeling from a sunburn. He sailed every weekend, he explained. His wife was also a doctor and they lived in Marblehead. The doctor in New York had spoken in a clipped tone. This Boston doctor, Dr. Squires, talked as if he were at a barbecue. His voice was upbeat and cheerful and he chuckled a lot. Howard kept expecting him to ask them if they wanted a hot dog or a hamburger. Dr. Squires told them about the house he and his wife had restored. They discovered a fireplace in the bedroom that had been completely covered up. Now it was in working order. Howard wondered if Elizabeth was like that fireplace. Perhaps Dr. Squires would discover something that the other doctor hadn't seen, and put her back in working order.

"It isn't good," Dr. Squires told them. "But I think radiation treatments may arrest it."

The doctor in New York had mentioned radiation. But his voice had offered no hope at all. "See a doctor in Boston," he had told them. Dr. Squires brought them a sense of hope. He ordered a CAT scan, more blood tests, and an appointment with a nutritionist. They would see him again in two days. Elizabeth had suggested they stay in Boston rather than drive back home. They left the doctor's office and walked out into the bright September sunlight. Everything seemed better. There were more tests, new doctors. Anything was possible. Howard felt that if he looked away from Elizabeth for a minute she might disappear. He tried this. He watched the traffic inch down the street, studied a car as someone tried to parallel-park. When Howard looked back at Elizabeth, she smiled at him and took his hand. She was still there. She had not vanished at all. He lifted her hand to his lips, and gently kissed it.

Howard and Elizabeth spent the two days until their next appointment wandering the streets of Boston. It was unseasonably warm for the middle of October. They pretended they were tourists. They walked the Freedom Trail, followed its crooked red path through the city streets. Elizabeth insisted on going inside the Old North Church. Howard waited on the sidewalk for her. When she came out, she smiled at him. "How about a pizza at the European?"

He agreed but felt angry at her for going into a church. Everything was going to be okay. She didn't need to ask for a little extra help. It's going to be okay, he thought for the hundredth—no, thousandth—time.

They walked hand in hand through the crowds at Quincy Market. Elizabeth bought some lemony potpourri for Rebekah and a Red Sox shirt for Jesse. They bought food at each stall they passed and then sat outside to eat it. For almost a month, Elizabeth had been consumed with her own mortality. She would lie in bed at night and picture the cancer growing inside of her. Now, after seeing Dr. Squires, she could at last see beyond that. She could pretend that they were on a little vacation. "We're here on vacation," she said to herself. "That's all."

After a while they walked to a small park near the

water. They sat on a bench. The air was salty and there were no crowds here, just a few people sitting on the grass reading or looking at the water. Elizabeth tossed peanuts to the gulls that circled nearby. She watched them pick up nuts in their mouths and fly away, into the sky. She followed one bird's flight until it disappeared into the clouds.

Dr. Squires's nose was peeling more heavily now. He greeted them with a smile. Elizabeth felt relaxed. There had been a mistake, she was sure.

"The news is good?" Howard asked.

Dr. Squires hesitated before he answered. "The progress of the disease seems to have slowed. Its early growth was apparently much more rapid."

"And?"

"I still recommend radiation. It may even arrest the growth altogether for a time."

Elizabeth felt weak. The pretending was over. Once more her life was being measured in terms of limited time.

"How long is a time?" Howard managed to say.

"I don't know," Dr. Squires said in his barbecue-host voice. "I've seen remissions that last as long as two or three years."

"What if there's no remission?" Elizabeth asked.

"There may very well be one."

"And there may not."

Dr. Squires nodded. "That's right. There may not."

The weather suddenly turned cool. As they drove west, toward home, they saw multi-colored leaves everywhere. It seemed as if the Mass Pike had been tie-dyed. They did not speak. Radiation treatments had been set up at a hospital closer to home, prescriptions had been filled.

Now they would go home and wait for a remission to happen. Or not.

As they pulled into the driveway with the rental car, Elizabeth said, "We have to tell them now."

Jesse ran out of the house.

"Neat car!" he shouted. "You look so funny driving, Dad."

Elizabeth put her arm around her son. He was ten, short for his age, his head a mass of black curls, his eyes clear blue.

"Rebekah was a real pain," he said as they went inside.

"Where is she?" Howard asked.

"I don't know. Reading somewhere. She wouldn't let me do anything at all. I was her prisoner. A slave."

Rebekah entered the kitchen then. Ever since she had sneaked off and had her nose fixed, Elizabeth was startled whenever she saw her. She looked younger with this new nose, her eyes seemed farther apart, her face thinner.

"Please don't ever leave me here alone with him again," she said. She was wearing one of Howard's sweaters and holding a library copy of *Princess Daisy*.

Elizabeth sank into a chair.

"A guy just called," Rebekah said. "Dr. Squires."

"A doctor," Jesse asked. "Who's sick?"

"I am," Elizabeth answered softly.

Only a week later and the children looked at Elizabeth as if she were a freak. Jesse kept reaching over and touching her hair, then quickly pulling his hand away. Rebekah sat far from her, as if the cancer were contagious. No one said the words cancer or dying out loud. No one said much of anything at all.

Elizabeth lay beside Howard in bed. She felt that her life was all behind her now. Nothing was definite or permanent anymore. There may or may not be a remission. In another year she might still be lying in this bed. Maybe she would be here in another two years. Or more. Or less. All the years leading up to this moment seemed like nothing. Growing up, meeting Howard, their life in New York, living on the farm, starting the pottery business, all of it added up to this moment, this time of lying here and trying not to die.

CLAUDIA, 1985

Claudia was under a tree at the bottom of the hill near the pond where Simon had drowned. Sometimes, if she lay real still—as she was now—she could actually hear the sounds of children laughing and splashing in the water. She could hear the boys, her sons, as they chased and teased Rebekah. Claudia could make herself believe that the sounds were real. She could picture herself in the kitchen of the farmhouse with Elizabeth. The two families still lived together in her daydreams. It is 1974, she imagines. Early summer. And she and Elizabeth are making a pesto sauce. As Claudia chops the dark green basil leaves, their rich smell is released and she inhales deeply. It is so good to be alive, she says.

Claudia liked to imagine she and Simon are having a picnic. The two of them used to sneak away together and go to the pond with a bag full of their favorite treats, things none of the others liked or food that didn't really go together—sweet gherkins, fig newtons, bananas, applesauce.

It was after these special picnics that Claudia had

taught Simon to swim. She had held him up by the waist as he kicked, his tanned legs splashing her. She had watched his head bob in the water, blowing a steady stream of bubbles. In her fantasy, Claudia warned Simon never to swim without her hands to hold him above water. She told him how special he was because, before she'd had him, she had been lost, really. It had been the feeling of him inside her that had given her a purpose. She told him all the things she had always felt about him but had never said because he was such a little boy, too young to understand.

Sometimes, though, she came to the pond and lay under the tree with her more than two feet of coppery hair fanned out around her and couldn't conjure these sounds or smells no matter how hard she tried. She could set the scene up: the farmhouse is red with rickety white shutters and the front yard is littered with bicycles and Nerf balls. The children are all around, running in for juice or a snack or to have a scraped knee kissed or an argument settled. There is the barn and Elizabeth is up in the loft painting. Howard and Claudia's husband, Peter, are working in the fields, figuring out an irrigation problem, maybe, or checking the corn. But sometimes, the scene, though completed in her mind, was more like one of those illustrations in a children's book that looks all right but asks: "What's wrong with this picture?" And on those days, the missing component was her inability to return with all of her senses to that time. She would set the scene but not be able to smell the air and hear all the right sounds or to feel, totally, the peace she had then.

It was that feeling, that complete picture, that Claudia went down to the pond to recapture. And on the days that she could return to that time, she would stay under the tree until it grew dark and someone—Peter, usually—came to get her. He would take her back to the house, no longer full of smells like fresh basil or cluttered with children's toys, emptied long ago of Elizabeth's family— Rebekah's hair ribbons and Elizabeth's paints and Howard's booming laugh. She sat at the table, unable then to reconcile the house in her mind with the cold, echoing place she sat in, and drank coffee with Peter. I was watching the children, she would say. They're swimming. And they're safe. Long ago, Peter had stopped explaining to her. He no longer even bothered to respond. Instead, he just looked away.

A lot happened on the day that Simon died. Howard left for Japan to study the Japanese technique of pottery making. Elizabeth found out that she was pregnant. And Nixon resigned as president. The day went like this: Claudia overslept. When she got downstairs, Elizabeth had already returned from taking Howard to the airport in Springfield. She was making curried egg salad for lunch. Rebekah was at the kitchen table, her hair in braids. Her overalls had a tiny stain on the bib.

Claudia had a lot to do. Peter was at an auction in Lee and so she had to pick the vegetables to bring to the market the next day. In those days she was a compulsive list-maker and she sat at the table with a pen and pad. The pad had CHEKHOV LISZT at the top of each page in big square letters.

"Why don't you go and play with the boys?" Elizabeth said to Rebekah. "You can bring them sandwiches and have a picnic."

Rebekah shrugged. She was a serious child with black hair and eyes that looked like black olives. She always wanted things she couldn't have. Her Christmas list the year before had blond hair and blue eyes at the top.

Just then, Claudia's three boys came in. They were all tall and thin with shaggy blond hair. Claudia called

47

them the Beach Boys. Sometimes they would put on a concert for her. Henry and Johnathan would strum imaginary guitars and Simon would keep the beat by banging his hands on any available tabletop. They would sing "Surfin' Safari" and "Help Me Rhonda," with Johnathan doing the high parts.

Now they came in for permission to go swimming in the pond. Claudia noticed that Simon's nose was sunburned. He had on a striped shirt with two little footprints on the pocket. Hang Ten. "I'll keep an eye on the little guys," he told her with a wink. He loved the role of big brother.

"How about some lunch first?" Elizabeth asked, and started making sandwiches for them. The curry made the egg salad a dark yellow. That color was etched in Claudia's mind forever. The next day she threw out some living room curtains that were the same rich gold.

"Can we eat under the tree?" Henry asked. He was only six then, but almost as tall as Simon.

"Sure," Claudia said. She put down her pen and helped Elizabeth wrap the sandwiches. She put some fruit in the bag for them too.

Johnathan insisted on carrying the food. He was always trying to prove he wasn't a baby anymore. "See," he said, "I can carry this by myself. I'm a big boy now."

Elizabeth persuaded Rebekah to go with them. As the children left, she shouted after them. "Don't swim right after you eat. You'll get a cramp."

"That's an old wives' tale, you know," Claudia laughed.

"Well," Elizabeth shrugged, "it can't hurt."

"My mother used to always warn me not to sit on the sidewalk. It gives you piles."

"Piles?"

"Hemorrhoids."

Both women laughed.

"It's such a funny day," Claudia said then.

"You slept too late."

"Mmmm. I had strange dreams. The tree near the pond was choking me, and Simon came to save me. Then we rode off on a porpoise."

They were silent for a moment.

"Did you ever wish," Claudia said, "I don't know . . . that things could stay the same?"

"Are you feeling blue because Howard went to Japan for that training?"

"I guess that's part of it. When he comes back you'll all move and start a pottery business. I don't know. I feel sort of like things will never be this good again. The way they are now."

Elizabeth put her hand over Claudia's. "My poor friend. You never did take to change very well. But it will be a while before we find a place where we can live and have room for a workshop and a store too."

Claudia smiled a little.

"All right," Elizabeth said. "I was saving this for more of a major announcement but, since you need some cheering up, I'll tell you now."

"If it'll cheer me up, I'm ready."

"I got a call today from the doctor. The rabbit died."

Claudia shrieked and the women hugged. Then suddenly, unexpectedly, Claudia began to cry.

"Happy tears," she said. "Honest."

Claudia considered, for a brief moment, abandoning her chores and going for a swim with the children. But it was already late and she had so much to do. Of course, had she gone, she would always think, Simon would not have died. She would have been there to save him. And

49

sometimes, in her daydreams under the tree, that is how the day went.

By the time Claudia was in the garden picking the vegetables, the sun was at its hottest. She still could easily recall how strong the smell of the dirt was in the noontime sun. It reminded her of her hometown in California. In Delano, the temperature would hit 100 degrees every day and bring the smell of hot dry dirt to her in the same way as today. Claudia thought of this as she picked first the tomatoes and then the radishes. She filled large baskets with the vegetables, heaping them so high that some tumbled to the ground. In the details that she could recall from the day that Simon died, the order in which she picked the vegetables and the way they looked was perhaps the strongest. The tomatoes were blood red, the radishes a brighter shade of red, almost magenta, and both were covered with dirt that allowed the colors just to peek through, like the vegetables in one of Elizabeth's paintings.

Claudia was pulling carrots out of the ground when she caught a glimpse of Rebekah going into the barn. A few minutes later, Rebekah and Elizabeth both emerged. Elizabeth waved over to her.

"The boys are teasing her," she shouted in explanation.

Claudia nodded and continued picking the carrots. It crossed her mind to go down to the pond and tell them to leave Rebekah alone. But she didn't.

It seemed like only a few minutes later, but by the slant of the sun and the number of filled baskets, Claudia realized it was actually an hour or more later that the commotion began.

First she heard shouting from down by the pond. She looked up, confused. For a moment she thought she really was back in Delano, a young girl again on her parents' farm. Once, there had been an accident there. A Mexican farm worker had gotten hurt in a piece of machinery. Claudia was about eleven at the time, and had stood, unable to move, as the frightened voices neared. "Señorita," they had shouted, "get help." But she had just stood there with the smell of dry dirt all around her and the hot sun beating down. And now, here was her son, Henry, running and shouting for help. Something terrible had happened. Claudia watched as Johnathan ran up the hill as well, howling like a hurt puppy. Yet she could see that he wasn't hurt at all. My God, she thought, it's Simon.

As if she were watching a movie run in slow motion, Claudia saw Elizabeth run out of the house with Rebekah and motion for all the children to stay, stay put. Don't go down there, Claudia told herself. The wind blew Elizabeth's hair into her face and she had to keep reaching up to pull it away so she could see as she ran. Johnathan was howling incoherently and Henry ran to the top of the hill, looked down, then ran back to the house, over and over he did this. At the top of the hill, as he peered down, he hopped on one foot, like he had to go to the bathroom.

Later, people told Claudia that she, too, had run down to the pond, right behind Elizabeth. They said that she had stood screaming at the edge of the water as Elizabeth pulled Simon out and tried to breathe life into him. But she was sure that they were wrong. She had stayed in the garden and picked the lettuce and then the summer squash. An ambulance came and still she kept picking. But don't you remember running up the hill, holding Simon's hand on the stretcher and Elizabeth yelling for the children to go inside the house? they asked her later. She had looked up, she remembered, when they put him in the ambulance, then she had resumed picking the summer squash. They, too, were a rich yellow. And it was then she had thought of the draperies in the living room. She didn't leave the garden until Elizabeth came and led her away. "No," they told her later. "You ran down to the pond and rode in the ambulance all the way to the hospital." But she shook her head.

Later, as they sat, numb and silent in the living room waiting for Peter to return from Lee, Howard called from Kennedy airport. His flight to Japan was delayed and, he told them, Richard Nixon had resigned.

Under the tree near the pond, Claudia was on her back and listening to the children's voices that only she could hear. The breeze made the leaves move in a kind of waltz. The branches of the tree were arms that reached out to her and picked her off the ground. Claudia smiled as Simon came and took her from the dancing tree and into his arms. He was tall and blond and so very strong. She waved good-bye to the tree.

"Simon," she whispered.

"No, Mom. It's Henry."

Claudia sighed. "I see."

He put her down gently, supported her on his arm.

"Can you walk okay?" he asked her.

Claudia nodded and they glided up the hill toward the house. She looked back at the pond and watched the boys splash in the water.

"Today," she said, "I picked all the vegetables. First the tomatoes, then radishes and carrots. Then lettuce, and finally, summer squash."

HENRY, 1985

If anyone were to notice the lanky blond boy and the bulkier dark-haired one sitting together hour after hour on Indian Rock in near silence, it would be inevitable to wonder what had brought them together. That was how unlikely a pair these two were. Henry looked like the boy on the beach who gets sand kicked in his face. Sometimes he wore small round wire-rimmed glasses. Always he carried a book with him. The other boy, Pogo, was the one who kicked sand in the boys like Henry's faces. He was not tall, but his muscles made up for his lack of height. He was described frequently as massive rather than merely large. In high school, he had been an All-State wrestler both his junior and senior years. The last book that Pogo read was *To Kill a Mockingbird* in eighth grade.

When he wasn't with Pogo, Henry sat in the loft in the barn and read. He also plotted how to get Rebekah Morgan to fall in love with him. Lately Henry fantasized that he was Jay Gatsby and Rebekah was Daisy, the distant streetlights in the town his green light. They lay ahead of him as symbols of his hope and love.

Pogo worked in Holyoke at a factory that made clothes for expensive teddy bears. He liked to sit in his '67 Mustang convertible and drink beer in the high school parking lot at night. Pogo was twenty years old, three years older than Henry. In October, he would marry his high school sweetheart, Carol. Carol was a cashier at the A&P. This summer she had been working extra hours and Saturdays to save money for their future.

It was a warm Saturday in June and Pogo and Henry were perched on Indian Rock. The afternoon sun was giving way to dusk, the sky growing pink around the edges.

Pogo sipped his beer.

"Sure is pretty," he said.

Henry didn't answer, just drew on the end of a joint he was smoking.

"We sure do live in a pretty corner of the world, huh?"

"I guess so," Henry said.

Pogo drained his can of beer.

"Shit," he said. "I've got to go pick up Carol at work." He crushed the can in his hand and tossed it downward. The sound of it as it bounced off the rocks echoed for quite some time.

"Why do you always litter?" Henry asked, shaking his head.

"It disintegrates. Really."

"No, it doesn't."

Pogo shrugged.

They sank back into their comfortable silence and watched the pink as it spread throughout the sky. It deepened, turned to violet, faded into smoky purple in the distance.

"I hear they've got some great sunsets in Hawaii," Pogo said.

"Sounds right."

"Yeah?"

"Well, the sun sets in the west."

"Right."

Henry nodded.

"Shit," Pogo said as he got up. "I'm late. You want to come with me to get Carol?"

Henry shrugged.

"Come on. Come with me."

"Okay," Henry said.

They made their way down the rocks. Henry stopped to pick up the crushed Miller cans. He threw them into the metal trash can on the corner near Pogo's car.

"Did you know," Henry said as they drove, "that I was almost on *That's Incredible?*"

"Get out."

"Really."

"Was it for some wild stunt? Like I saw a guy once that put on a special suit that wouldn't burn, you know, like it was treated with some special stuff. And he put this suit on and he ran through a tunnel of fire. It was really something. Flames shooting out everywhere. And the suit was on fire but I guess like it didn't really burn, you know. These guys ran out and hosed him down. For a while it looked like maybe he *did* burn anyway. He just lay there in this like burned-up suit and John Davidson got real nervous. His voice was all shaky and stuff. But then the guy jumps up and tears the suit off. It was so great."

"Well, it wasn't for anything like that."

"Another time, right? I saw this guy who was like blind and retarded and maybe even deaf and these real old people adopted him. So they were sleeping one night and the old lady thinks maybe she left the radio on or something because she hears music. So she goes downstairs and it's the retarded guy playing the piano and singing 'Amazing Grace'!"

"An idiot savant."

"Whatever."

Henry laughed. He liked being high and riding through the warm evening with Pogo.

They parked in front of the A&P and waited for Carol. The store lights were bright and Henry watched the people inside. There was a pregnant woman in the express lane with two baskets of food. The people in line behind her were staring and pointing because she had much more than the ten-item limit. A tall man wearing pink glasses and a toupee and holding two frozen dinners started counting the items in her baskets. Henry could see them clearly as they rolled down the conveyor belt. Froot Loops. Oreos. Pampers.

A boy in a green smock was collecting shopping carts in the parking lot. When he had a line of them, he wheeled them through the mechanical doors and into the store. Henry watched the boy add these carts to a line already inside. The doors opened again like a large toothless mouth and Carol walked out with another girl. They both had on tight jeans and high-heeled sandals. Their eyes were rimmed in bright blue, their lips were red and shiny.

"That's Debbie," Pogo said. "Boy, is she hot."

Henry looked at the girl as she approached. She had on a white muscle T-shirt. Her breasts showed through, large and heavy. Pogo was always trying to fix Henry up with someone. He couldn't understand why Henry wasted his time on Rebekah Morgan.

Henry moved to the backseat so that Carol could sit next to Pogo. As soon as the girls got in, they lit up cigarettes.

"This is Henry, Debbie," Carol said.

"Hi." Debbie smiled. "Hi, Pogo." She tugged on Pogo's hair.

"Get out," he said. "I'm driving."

"What a day," Carol said.

"I'll say," Debbie agreed. "I hate working customer service. Why does Eddie put me there every Saturday?"

"The same reason he puts me on Express. There are always fights in Express. Every single time. There's always some sleazy person who has like a million items and comes through Express. Can't these people read?"

"Some lady today comes up to the window with this can of string beans and shoves it right in my face. 'Look at what's in here,' she says."

"God!" Carol said, turning around toward the back-seat. "What was it?"

"A huge bug. I mean huge."

"God! How gross." Carol turned back around.

"You're telling me. I thought I was going to barf. I mean this huge bug was right in my face."

"Carol," Pogo said, "stop talking and open some brews."

"Did you get Lite?" she asked.

"I told you before that Lite tastes like piss."

"God! You got Miller."

Carol opened the beers and gave everybody one.

"I ask you this one little thing and you can't do it," Carol said. "I'm trying to lose weight for the wedding. I want to look good, Pogo, for that one day. It's only the most important day of my entire life."

Henry sipped his beer. He wished he had gone straight home. Beside him, Debbie had finished her cigarette and was snapping a piece of gum. She caught him looking at her and smiled.

"That must have been really disgusting," he said.

57

She looked puzzled. "What?"

"Those string beans. With the bug."

"Oh, that. Let me tell you something. That no-name brand stuff always has bugs or hairs in it. I work Customer Service practically every Saturday. I know."

Henry nodded.

"Ooooo," Carol shrieked. *"Back to the Future."*

Henry looked at where she was pointing. They were passing the multiplex cinema. A brightly lit rotating sign listed the six movies that were playing there. Steven Spielberg's *Back to the Future* was at Cinemas 3 and 4.

"Let's go, Pogo," Carol said in a little girl voice.

"I don't want to see that shit."

"Pleeeease." Then in her normal voice, "Debbie, do you want to see it?"

"I'm dying to see it."

"See, Pogo."

"All right. All right."

As they waited in line, Henry realized that Debbie, who was playing Donkey Kong with Carol, expected him to buy her ticket as well.

"Pogo," Henry said, "I've only got a couple bucks. I didn't know I was going on a date, for Christ's sake."

"That's okay. I'll cover you. I'm telling you, she's hot."

As they walked into the movie, Carol stopped and pointed to one of the framed prints that lined the lobby's walls.

"Isn't that adorable, Debbie."

Her finger rested on the edge of a Norman Rockwell print of two children and a dog gazing at a huge yellow moon.

Debbie snapped her gum. "Adorable."

"Pogo, we have to start getting stuff for an apartment. I mean, the wedding's only four months away."

"Don't remind me," he whispered to Henry.

Henry hated the movie. Around him in the theater, the audience laughed and applauded. He looked at Debbie, smiling and cracking her gum, mesmerized by what was happening on the screen. What am I missing? he thought. Why don't I understand this movie?

"How can I give you a Tab when you haven't even ordered yet?" the man in the movie said. The audience roared with laughter.

"God," Debbie said to Henry, "a Tab. I love it."

He smiled at her. Stupid, he thought. This movie is so stupid.

"That movie," Debbie said later as they ate ice cream at Friendly's, "was really incredible."

"I want to see it again," Carol said.

"Definitely."

"Did you ever see *Invasion of the Body Snatchers*?" Henry asked Debbie.

"What?"

"*Invasion of the Body Snatchers*. These alien pods—"

"*Alien*. I saw *Alien*. That was so great."

"God!" Carol said. "Remember when that guy's stomach exploded?"

"That was so gross," Debbie agreed.

"I'm trying to eat some ice cream here," Pogo said. "Do you mind?"

After they left Friendly's, they drove to the old high school football field. Now the town had a new high school and a sports complex. The old school was turned into a home for senior citizens and the football field remained deserted, overgrown with weeds and litter.

Carol and Pogo went behind the bleachers with a blanket, a radio, and a six-pack. Henry and Debbie sat on the ten-yard line.

"Do you want to smoke a joint?" Henry asked after a time.

"Sure."

As they smoked, Debbie talked about high school. She graduated last year, she told him. "I really miss it," she said. "It was so great. You know, something going on every night. Of course, I had a steady boyfriend the whole four years. We broke up though. Rick Carrerro? You know him?"

Henry shook his head.

"Hey. Where did you go to school? I don't remember you at all."

"I didn't go." Henry shifted uncomfortably, avoided Debbie's question, Didn't go to school?

Henry could accept the oddities of his family: a silent father who spent many nights away from home, a mother who escaped into near lunacy in order to avoid the guilt she felt over the death of her first son, a decade ago; a younger brother, Johnathan, who was a mnemonic genius, rattling off entire Shakespeare plays and Eliot's "The Waste Land." It was this brother who almost got the entire family on *That's Incredible*. The *Boston Globe* story about them had carried a line about Johnathan's talent and caught the attention of the show's producer. However, his mother had backed off at the last minute in one of her more lucid moments, telling the show's representatives: "We're not freaks, you know."

Pogo never asked about the eccentricities of Henry's family. The two could sit in near silence, breaking the quiet sporadically to make observations about love or life while avoiding the step that would have them cross from pals to great friends. Other friends had stared at Henry's mother's two-foot-long hair and curled fingernails in horror. Once, a boy had actually run away screaming as Henry's mother groped at him, calling for her dead son.

But Pogo, who rarely visited the farm at all, never asked Henry about her or stared. He sometimes asked Johnathan to recite something and would sit listening in awe.

And, Henry knew, perhaps part of his love for Rebekah could be attributed to her familiarity with all of these things. She was one of the few people who remembered his mother from before Simon died, from the nearly idyllic time their two families shared life together on the farm. No one else could recall with him a time when his mother had been the best Nerf-ball pitcher around or the day she had jumped into the pond fully clothed for a swim with all the kids.

Suddenly, thinking of Rebekah, Henry had the urge to talk to her. He wished she were with him now instead of this gum-snapping, large-breasted girl. He looked at Debbie. She seemed to be waiting for something. An answer? A question? A kiss?

"That's pretty weird," she said. "I mean, not going to school."

He kissed her in hopes of silencing her. Debbie's lipstick was sweet, flavored strawberry, or cherry, perhaps. He couldn't decide which. She thrust her tongue into his mouth immediately. It darted back and forth, scraped against his teeth, and pushed against his gums. Inside, beyond the berry-flavored lips, there was the taste of spearmint gum and stale cigarettes. Pogo had told Henry that she was hot. They kissed in this manner for a few minutes, and then he touched her breast. She pushed against him. She *is* hot, he thought, and tugged at her T-shirt. Her breasts fell loose from it. Just as he began to kiss them she shouted and pulled away from him.

"Jesus! What the hell do you think you're doing? What exactly did Pogo say about me?"

Henry stared at her.

"I thought you were different. Sensitive. I mean, I

61

opened up to you. Do you think I tell everyone about missing school and stuff? Jesus!"

Debbie walked quickly back to the car and Henry followed close behind. When they reached the Mustang, she leaned on the horn, some secret signal that called Carol to her rescue.

Henry entered Rebekah's kitchen. She and her mother were making a salad.

"Hi!" her mother said to him. "Grab a knife and start chopping. We put everyone who walks in here to work."

"I brought these," he said, and handed the bouquet of wildflowers to no one in particular.

Elizabeth took them. "Aren't these pretty, Rebekah?"

Rebekah looked up for the first time and Henry's breath caught in his throat. Her black hair was frizzy from the humidity. She was wearing a baggy blue plaid jumper. It was cotton and, despite its size, stuck to her because of the heat.

"Gorgeous," she said sarcastically.

You, too, he thought. You are gorgeous too. He picked up the knife her mother was using and began to cut some cucumbers.

"Can you stay for lunch?" Elizabeth asked.

"Sure." He smiled at Rebekah. "Howard said I could borrow a couple of books."

"He's not here, but go on and poke through the bookshelves."

"I've been reading a lot of Fitzgerald lately. Have you read *Great Gatsby*, Rebekah?"

"Seventeen times."

"Rebekah's in her Judith Krantz phase," Elizabeth said.

"I'm filling my mind with trash. Torrid sex scenes, breasts like rosebuds, his manhood throbbing—"

Elizabeth laughed. "She's impossible, Henry."

"Impossible, yes. Hungry, no. Everything's ready for you. I'm going for a walk."

Henry's heart collapsed as he watched her walk out the door.

"I just don't see what you see in her. She looks like she just wandered out of an old attic or something."

Pogo and Henry were at the quarry, lying naked on the rocks that surrounded the water.

"And what about Debbie?" Pogo continued.

"What about her?"

"She likes you. She told Carol she really likes you."

"I want Rebekah."

"But she doesn't want you. And believe me, you don't want her to want you. Do you know that I spent the entire night last night listening to Carol and her mother talk about color schemes. It was so fucking boring. You know, Henry, I wish I had the balls to leave."

"Leave? Leave Carol?" Henry sat up.

"Leave this whole fucking town. I don't know. I lived here my whole life. I mean, where else is there to go? Shit. I've known Carol since I was fourteen."

Henry didn't answer. This didn't seem right. How fragile was love, he thought, that someone can want to leave the girl he's been with since he was fourteen years old?

"I heard," Pogo said, "that in Hawaii all the girls are hot. You know, begging for it. There are palm trees and like fruit growing everywhere. You can walk down the street with a little hula dancer on your arm and pick like a peach or something right there."

It sounded to Henry like the thought of palm trees and peaches was more exciting to Pogo than Carol. Pogo had never sounded quite this way before.

"Hey," Pogo said as he sat up, "you want one of those bears?"

"What bears?"

"One of the fancy teddy bears. For Rebekah. I mean, those things sell for like fifty bucks."

"The bears from where you work?"

"Yeah. Those bears. Like, there's one dressed in a trench coat and he's called Humphrey Beargot after some old actor. And there's another one in a ballet suit named Bearishnakov after some fag Russian ballerina. So what does she like? Movies? Dancing?"

Henry shrugged.

"I'm telling you, she'll love it. There's all kinds too."

"I don't have fifty dollars."

"Did I say I wanted fifty bucks?" Pogo lay back down. "Man, can you imagine being in Hawaii? I'd get a surfboard and catch a wave and ride to all the islands there. Or Australia. Like in *Endless Summer*."

What about Carol? Henry thought. What about the Norman Rockwell picture of the boy and the girl and the dog?

On the way home, in the Mustang with the top down and Pogo tapping on the steering wheel in time with the Talking Heads, Henry began to feel guilty. Hell, he thought, maybe Pogo doesn't love Carol at all. Why should Henry be upset if all Pogo wanted to do was go to Hawaii and surf?

"You know what?" Henry blurted out. "When I was six my big brother died. We were swimming and he drowned. Right there beside me."

When he said this they had reached the farm. He pointed in the direction of the pond. "We were swimming right down there."

"No shit," Pogo said.

They sat in the car, in front of the house. Henry's

heart was racing. Right after Simon died, Henry would walk up to people and say, "My brother died, you know." But it had been years since he had said those words to anyone. Sometimes at night he woke up from a dream in which he was the one drowning and Simon was drying off on the grass, his image growing more and more blurry as Henry sank deeper into the sand.

He looked over at Pogo now. This former All-State wrestler who loaded boxes of well-dressed bears was a most unlikely confidant. Perhaps, Henry thought, he had said too much. He had spent so much time surrounded by silence and dreams, he was not sure what to say or when to say it.

His mother opened the door. She was very thin. From here, with her hair all around her, she looked like an oversized Raggedy Ann doll.

"Henry?" she called.

"Yeah, it's me."

"Who are you sitting with in that car?"

"Pogo. Remember Pogo?"

"Well, why don't you come in?"

Pogo touched Henry's arm. He was surprisingly gentle for someone so large. "Is that why she's that way?" he asked. "Because of your brother?"

Henry nodded.

"Let's go inside," Pogo said. "I'm pretty thirsty."

"Well . . ."

"I'll leave as soon as I have some soda or something."

Henry's mother smiled at them when they came inside.

"You remember Pogo, Ma?"

"No," she said sadly. "But it's very nice to meet you."

"We're just going to get something cold to drink," Henry explained.

He led Pogo to the kitchen and was surprised when he saw that his mother had followed them.

"Johnathan made lemonade," she said. "Minute Maid."

"Sounds good," Pogo said as he sat at the table.

Henry was aware of how rundown the house was—curtainless windows and warped linoleum. He got three Flintstones jelly glasses and filled them with lemonade.

"I have never known anyone named Pogo," his mother said.

Henry was too tense to sit. Instead, he leaned against the sink. His mother seemed more lucid than usual, her eyes only slightly foggy.

"It's just a nickname," Pogo said.

She smiled.

"My real name is Ralph."

"Oh!" she said, as if everything were suddenly very clear.

"Thanks for the lemonade, Mrs. Collier." Pogo got up, stretched.

"Please," she said, standing too, "don't go yet. Stay for dinner."

Henry flinched. His mother had not made dinner in years. The last time she tried, she had started a fire in the oven. Pogo looked at Henry for his okay.

"Ma," Henry said, "I don't think Pogo can stay."

Her face clouded over. "Please stay."

"Well," Pogo said, "well, sure. Okay."

"Oh, good! Now, you boys sit in the living room while I get everything ready."

When they got into the living room, Johnathan was there, sitting on the sofa reading *The New Yorker*.

"Hi, Romeo," Pogo greeted him.

"You want some Romeo?" Johnathan threw the magazine down and adjusted his thick Buddy Holly glasses. " 'Oh, she doth teach the torches to burn bright, it seems she hangs upon the cheek of night Like a rich jewel in an Ethiop's ear. Beauty too rich for use, for earth too dear!' ''

"Phew!" Pogo said, and shook Johnathan's hand. "That was beautiful."

"I'm learning the histories now," Johnathan said.

"I like Romeo best," Pogo said softly.

Finally, their mother announced that dinner was ready. In the kitchen, each place had silverware and napkins at it but no plates. Henry paused, wondering whether to say something or ignore it.

"Now," she said, potholders in hand, "we have turkey with giblet gravy, fried chicken, or Salisbury steak."

Johnathan and Henry exchanged nervous glances.

"Which would you like, Pogo?" she asked.

"The steak, please."

She opened the oven and revealed four TV dinners. "Here we go." She placed a steaming one in front of Pogo. "Who wants fried chicken?" Henry accepted the tin plate she offered to him, all the compartments filled with flat food.

"There," she said smiling. "Now, isn't this nice?"

The town was having a fireworks display at the new high school. Its parking lot was sandwiched between the town below and the Berkshires above. Henry had agreed to go with Pogo, Carol, and Debbie. Three days before, he had received a card with a picture of a couple holding hands as they walked on a moonlit beach. Inside, in gold and purple ink was a note from Debbie:

Dear Henry,

It's 1985 so it should be OK for a girl to send a boy a card even if he hasn't called her or anything. I thought you were nice and I hope we can be friends at least.

Sincerely,
Debbie

Now the four of them sat on a blanket and waited for the fireworks to begin. Debbie was wearing red shorts and a white halter top. "Do I look patriotic?" she had asked Henry as he slid into the car beside her. She snuggled up to him then and had remained close ever since.

Carol kept talking about the wedding. Debbie was a bridesmaid and they described her gown in great detail— the pleats, the fabric, the straps and ruffles and matching headpiece. Pogo looked miserable.

As Debbie was talking, Henry became aware of familiar voices beside him. He turned and saw Rebekah and her family sitting nearby on a large Mexican blanket. What is she doing here? he thought in horror. Debbie was clinging to his arm like a tick, smiling and snapping gum. Perhaps he shouldn't have thanked her for the card. Perhaps he shouldn't have told her that of course they were more than just friends.

Rebekah was wearing the same baggy plaid jumper that she wore the last time he saw her. She looked bored. And beautiful. He knew he couldn't let her see him with Debbie. It could ruin any chance he had to win her affection.

Henry laughed nervously, then whispered, "Hey. Maybe we'd see better if we sat over there." He pointed to some vague distant area.

"Move?" Debbie giggled. "Why?"

"I think we'd see better."

"They're fucking fireworks," Pogo said. "They're in the sky. We can't miss them."

Debbie squeezed his arm. "Silly," she whispered into his ear.

Henry glanced nervously at the Morgans. He wished he could become invisible. What, he wondered, would Jay Gatsby do in this predicament? Before he had time to imagine, he was spotted by Rebekah's brother.

"Henry's here! Look!" Jesse shouted. "Hi, Henry."

Howard and Elizabeth looked over. They waved and smiled politely. Are they thinking I'm a traitor for being here with someone other then Rebekah? he wondered. They must know I still love her. More.

"Who's your girlfriend?" Rebekah asked.

Henry saw Elizabeth nudge her to stop. He smiled over at them blankly.

"I'm Debbie DeSimone," Debbie said possessively. "I know you from school." She was holding Henry's arm with both of her hands. "I graduated last year," she added in a superior voice.

Henry continued to smile at the Morgans.

"What's wrong, Henry?" Rebekah asked. "Can't you talk?"

"Happy Fourth of July," he said, and the fireworks began.

"That is some girlfriend you've got there," Rebekah said to Henry on the telephone.

"She isn't my girlfriend. I was with a group of people."

"Two couples is a group?"

"I didn't call to discuss this," Henry said.

"I'm very busy, Henry. I have a lot on my mind. If you want to borrow another book from my father, just come over and get it."

"I didn't call for that."

"What is this, a game, Henry?"

"No, no, not at all. I . . . I thought you might like to,

to . . . do something. With me. I can get a car. A great car. A convertible. We could go to a concert or a play or—"

"Henry, forget it. Take your girlfriend."

"She's not—"

"Good-bye, Henry." She hung up.

"I am so miserable," Henry moaned. He and Pogo were lying on the rocks at the quarry. The sun was so hot they had to keep jumping into the water to cool off. "I offered her a concert, a play—anything. And she turned me down. No excuse or anything."

"You think you're miserable?" Pogo asked, staring up at the sky. "I feel like I'm in one of those rooms like Indiana Jones. You know, they keep getting smaller and smaller. The walls and the ceiling and stuff keep moving in." He sat up and Henry noticed that Pogo's body was not as firm as it had been just a few months earlier. His muscles were sagging, turning to flab. "When I'm with Carol, I can't even breathe."

In the past month, the comfortable silence they had established began to disappear. In its place was the kind of talk new friends often have, an almost urgent attempt to learn everything about each other. Henry had told Pogo about his brother and the day he died. He had explained how his life had changed since then and what it had been like before. He had told him all about Rebekah.

Pogo talked mostly about wrestling, how it felt to pin someone, to win, and—most of all—what it was like to be chosen for the All-State team. Pogo also spoke of Carol. "She's the only girl I ever did with it," he said. "Shit, man," he had told Henry, "I've got to marry her."

Now Henry sat up and said, "Why don't you go to Hawaii?"

"Shit," Pogo said.

"I mean it."

Pogo shook his head. "I've lived here my whole life. That means something, you know. I've lived in this town my whole fucking life."

It was quiet for a moment, then Pogo said, "Man, you know that in Hawaii there are all kinds of jobs? Outdoor jobs year-round. No packing fucking teddy bears into boxes all day."

Henry nodded.

"Hey, did you ever find out what kind of stuff Rebekah likes? You know, so I can get you one of those bears to give her."

"Pogo, she won't even talk to me."

"Shit. And Carol won't shut up."

The two lay back down. After a time Pogo said, "Fucking Hawaii."

It was the first week in August, the air was hot and thick in the way it got around that time of year. Henry was reading in the barn when Johnathan came in, barechested and barefoot.

"There's someone here to see you."

Henry looked up from the book. "Pogo?"

"Not unless he's grown breasts. Huge breasts."

"Debbie." The name was barely out of his mouth when she appeared at the door. Just two nights earlier they had double-dated again and this time, at the old football field, she had offered very little resistance. "We can't go all the way," she had whispered. But now, seeing her in the barn, Henry wondered if going almost all the way was against the law. He looked behind her for an angry policemen or a father with a shotgun.

"Do you know where Pogo is?" she demanded.

This was about Pogo, Henry thought with relief. He shrugged.

"Hawaii!" she shouted. "He left Carol and went to Hawaii!"

Henry jumped up. "What?" He felt elated, ecstatic. "He went to Hawaii?"

"Everything's off," Debbie said. "The wedding and everything. All their plans are off. Kaput. Can you believe it?"

"He really did it," Henry said, almost to himself. Then, louder, "He really did it."

"You knew he was going? What kind of person are you? Did you know he was going to Hawaii? You knew and you never said a word to anyone? Did you know it the other night? Huh?"

Henry wanted to shout with joy. Pogo was gone, free.

"You are a low and sleazy person, Henry," Debbie shouted. "You are slime. My best friend Carol is at home crying her heart out. That's something for you to live with, you asshole."

She turned to leave but stopped at the door. "He left something for you. A box. A huge box. To think I lugged it over here for you." Then she screamed, "You're not even upset!"

After she was gone, Johnathan and Henry ran outside and opened the box.

"It's full of bears!" Johnathan said with a mixture of awe and puzzlement.

They pulled the well-dressed teddy bears out one at a time, studying each one. There was one in gray flannel called Bearman of the Board, a Civil War Belle called Scarlette O'Beara, and William Shakesbear and Lionel Bearrymore. Henry scooped up an armful.

"Let's go," he said to Johnathan.

"Where?"

"Bring the bears!" Henry shouted as he began to run off.

"Where?"

"To Rebekah's!"

SPARROW, 1985

"Maybe I'll go to college in Maine," Sparrow said.

She stood with her back to her mother, looking out the window. The air-conditioner sent cold air up at her, blowing her hair in her face.

Suzanne had brought home paperwork, a client's investment portfolio to look over. She had papers spread all over the dining room table.

"This man's money is in all the wrong places," she said.

"I mean, once you and Ron are married, you won't want me around anymore."

"That kind of talk is ridiculous. Foolish."

"It won't matter where I go to school. I could go to Alaska."

"I doubt there's a school you'd be interested in in Alaska."

"So I might as well go where I have family."

Suzanne sighed.

Sparrow watched the sailboats on the bay. Her mother was with Ron all the time. Almost every weekend they went to look for a summer house to buy. Martha's Vineyard. Marblehead. Newport. Her mother was more tanned than Sparrow had ever seen her. There were freckles across the bridge of her nose. The sun had bleached her hair a whitish-blond.

"We're going to Watch Hill this weekend," Suzanne said.

Sparrow heard papers shuffle behind her.

"Why don't you come with us, just this once?" her mother asked.

Sparrow shook her head.

"You're not even trying," Suzanne said.

"It would be," Sparrow said, "incredibly boring."

"We're staying at a big old hotel that sits way up high and overlooks the ocean. Ron said that it's really quite lovely."

"I'm sure it is." Sparrow turned from the window. "Since when are you such a beach bum?" she asked. "In my entire life I think we spent one weekend on Cape Cod with some client of yours. And once we had dinner at The Barnacle in Marblehead. That's it. And then that one time I was little and we—"

"We want to buy a summer house," her mother said quickly, looking down at the papers before her.

"What's next? Are you going to get a Mustang convertible and cruise Revere Beach?"

"I would think you'd be excited."

"I am," Sparrow said dryly. "Thrilled."

"You haven't even given Ron a chance. It took me a long time to meet someone like him, you know. It took a long time for me to get here."

Sparrow looked at her mother.

"I don't even know my real father," she said. "You want me to pretend Ron is my father."

"That just isn't true, Susan. But I am marrying Ron

and we will all be living here together. It would be a lot easier if you would accept that and forget about the past.''

"How can I forget what I don't even know?"

Her mother sighed and looked down. She picked up a paper from the table.

"This man," she said, spreading her hands out over the papers, "has one hundred thousand dollars in a regular checking account." She laughed. "Not even a NOW account."

"Ron is not my father," Sparrow said.

She turned and looked out the window again. She had a fantasy of her and her mother, giggling and smoking cigarettes, maybe even dancing the twist. There was a man in the background, watching them and smiling. He had dark blond hair and a droopy moustache. He was her father.

The night before they went to Watch Hill, Sparrow had dinner with her mother and Ron at a Mexican restaurant called GuadalaHarry's. Ron let Sparrow choose the restaurant. They sat amid the phony Mexican tiles and loud barroom laughter. Her mother allowed Sparrow to order a frozen strawberry margarita. It came in a huge glass rimmed with sugar. Sparrow's mother ordered an extra dry Beefeater martini with a twist, but Ron laughingly ordered a margarita. "On the rocks," he said as he eyed the oversize frozen drinks around him. "Extra salt."

Suzanne looked at Sparrow and smiled secretively. "See?" she mouthed over the salt shaker.

"Isn't this place something?" he asked after their drinks arrived. "And the menu! This menu is really something." Ron pointed to the food descriptions, sagas of how Harry got the recipes, as he spoke.

"Have you been here before?" Suzanne asked Sparrow.

"I'm sure she has," Ron said. "Haven't you?"

Sparrow looked at the menu.

"I mean, it's such a fun place for a teenager," Ron continued. "Not that it isn't fun for old folks like us too," he added, squeezing Suzanne's shoulder.

Suzanne picked up a tortilla chip and sniffed it, then broke it in two, and frowned.

"Stale," she said. She took a small bite, then put it down.

"We'll get a fresh batch," Ron said.

"No," Suzanne said, "that's not necessary. Really."

Ron picked up the basket of chips and waved it at a waiter.

"Ron," Sparrow said, "put that down. You're embarrassing me."

"You know," Suzanne said, "Ron always makes a point of getting the proper treatment in restaurants. And I think he's right. People can really be so lax if you let them be. Like the wine. Remember that, Ron?"

"Absolutely," he said, still waving the basket. "We had a waiter—where was that, Suzanne? Up in Ipswich? We sent back a bottle of wine that tasted acidic and this waiter said the wine was fine, that it was our palate that was tainted from the garlic in our appetizer. Can you imagine?"

"Mushrooms stuffed with snails," Suzanne said.

"We sent for the manager and of course he was quite apologetic and replaced the bottle with a good one." Ron leaned toward Sparrow. "It's never too early to learn these things," he said.

Suzanne smiled at him.

"I think it's obnoxious," Sparrow said.

"Obnoxious to expect good service and fine food?" her mother said.

Ron stood up and snapped his fingers. "Excuse me," he said.

Sparrow held the large menu open in front of her face. "I can't believe this," she said.

The waiter stood behind Sparrow. She could smell the garlic and onions on him.

"These chips," Ron said, "are cold and stale."

The waiter didn't answer.

"I really don't believe this," Sparrow said.

"We'd like some fresh ones," Ron said. "And I think—correct me if I'm wrong—that they should be served warm."

"This isn't Maison Robert, for God's sake," Sparrow said.

"Good man," Ron said.

Sparrow wasn't sure, but she thought he slapped the waiter on the back.

"I believe this is Tex-Mex," Sparrow's mother said. "Yes. Tex-Mex. Not authentic." Then she added quickly, "Which is a nice change." The waiter put down a new basket of chips.

"Where was it," Ron said, "that we had that wonderful chicken mole, Suzanne?"

"I can't recall. Somewhere in Cambridge?"

Ron and her mother had their heads bent together as if that would increase their brain power.

"Susan," Ron said, "mole is an authentic Mexican sauce which, oddly enough, has chocolate as its base. It's quite delicious."

"Sol Aztec!" her mother announced triumphantly.

"Disgusting," Sparrow said as she dipped a corn chip into the overly sweet sauce. "It sounds disgusting."

"I can't wait for you to see it," her mother said. "Eleven fireplaces! A sweeping view. A panoramic view actually. And Susan, what a lovely view it is."

Sparrow looked out the window of Ron's BMW. The three of them—Sparrow, Suzanne, and Ron—were driving south on 95. Her mother and Ron had bought the house in Watch Hill. What a way to end the summer, her mother said when they started out today. Beside Sparrow, on the floor in the backseat was a cooler full of six-ounce bottles of Perrier. They were flavored—orange, lime, lemon.

"Rhode Island," Sparrow said.

"Home of Brown University," Ron said.

"An excellent school," her mother added.

"Do they have a good English department, Mom? Because I'm going to be a writer. A poet."

"A poet does not make money," her mother said sharply. "It's not a career."

"I think what your mother means," Ron said, "is that writing poems is more of a hobby. Something to do in your spare time."

"Really, Ron?" Sparrow said, her eyes locking with his in the rearview mirror. "I thought I'd write poems for a living and play with investing in my spare time. You know, for fun."

"I see," Ron laughed stiffly. "The joke's on me."

"There's this little place," Suzanne said, "where they make their own ice cream."

"Your mother had a triple scoop. What flavor was that, Suzanne? The one you liked so well?"

"Blueberry. Wait until you taste this ice cream."

Sparrow leaned back in the seat and sipped some orange Perrier.

"Be careful back there," Ron said. "Don't spill anything on the upholstery."

"I love when people get new cars," Sparrow muttered. "They get so paranoid."

Suzanne and Ron glanced at each other.

"I know," her mother said. "He won't let me smoke in here. He says that ruins the upholstery."

But Sparrow saw that she smiled at Ron when she said it.

The house was oversized, covered in weathered shingles and full of glass, so that the ocean could be seen from every room.

"We still need a lot of furniture," Suzanne said, gazing out toward the water. "That will be our winter project. In fact, you can pick out the room you want to be yours and fix it up any way you'd like. You can choose the colors, the furniture, everything. How does that sound?"

Sparrow stood beside her mother in the living room. The large glass doors were open and the air was thick with salt. Below them, waves crashed against the rocks. Ron had gone to the supermarket. We need provisions, he said when he left. We're really roughing it out here. With him gone, Sparrow felt more relaxed. She couldn't imagine really living with him. Maybe her mother would change her mind.

Suzanne sighed. "The ocean has always had a way of relaxing me. All those years of working so hard. There were times when I wished you and I could run away and camp out on a beach somewhere. Look for seagulls and driftwood. But, see, now, it was all worth it. All the planning and working and look what we've got." She opened her arms as if to embrace the ocean.

Sparrow looked at her mother. Her eyes looked as blue as the water she stretched her arms out to.

"I've got a great idea," Sparrow said. "Drop Ron and you and I will move here alone. Or maybe with someone different." She thought of the picture of her father.

Her mother ignored her. "It brings out the best in me," she said. "I just remembered something," she laughed. "Let me see if I can get it right. It's been a long time. 'The fish is—' no, 'The fish when she's exposed to air. Displays no trace of savoir-faire. But near the sea regains her balance. And exploits all her womanly talents.' Something like that."

They laughed together.

"Did you make that up, Mom?"

"Oh, no. It's Ogden Nash."

"When did you learn it?"

"Oh, I don't know. A long time ago someone used to say it to me."

"Who?"

"You know, even when you were a little girl, this big, you would ask a million questions. Who? Why? When?"

"Who?" Sparrow asked again.

"Nobody you know," her mother said.

In bed that night, Sparrow listened to the drone of Ron and her mother's voices. She couldn't make out their words. The air that came in through the window was wet and vaguely familiar.

Sparrow looked up at the ceiling. She could just make out the elaborate molding that bordered the edges, the blurred shape of acorns. Sometimes, like earlier tonight, she felt so close to her mother. Now Ron was with her, in the way. Once they were married, it would never be the same again. Sparrow closed her eyes. She thought about running away, going to Maine and finding her father. That would be her real family then. And everything would be all right.

PART TWO

BACK THEN

SUZANNE, CLAUDIA, AND ELIZABETH, 1966

C laudia was the one who had come all the way from California with her clothes in a pack on her back. She was full of stories about San Francisco. That first night, she sat cross-legged on her bed in the dorm room dressed in faded jeans and a patchwork vest, her dark red hair frizzing out past her shoulders, and faced her new roommate, Suzanne, telling her about her adventures in Haight-Ashbury that summer.

"Six of us lived in this great apartment right in the Haight," Claudia said. "Above a head shop."

Suzanne frowned, afraid to ask exactly what one bought in a head shop. Wigs? Hats? Shrunken heads?

"You know," Claudia said, "they sell papers, pipes, stuff like that."

Suzanne nodded, but she had no idea what this girl was talking about. She should have roomed with someone from her high school, she thought. Her parents were wrong. "You must expand your horizons," they had told her. "Meet new people." She looked at the tall bony girl sitting across from her and knew that she did not want to meet anyone else. Her horizons were expanded enough, thank you.

"Anyway," Claudia continued, "I was sort of living with this one guy, Bo, but this is the really incredible thing—I was with Bo but with everyone else too. And every day was glorious. Have you ever been to California?"

"Disneyland," Suzanne said, thinking that perhaps it wasn't too late to go to the housing office and request a room change.

Claudia laughed. "Disneyland! Well, this was sort of like Disneyland. Like a whole summer spinning around in one of those giant pink teacups. Have you ever done mushrooms?"

Suzanne smoothed the pleats on her skirts, thought of her mother's dinner parties—beef Wellington, asparagus vinaigrette, sauteed mushrooms in white wine. "Do the mushrooms for me, will you, Suzanne?" Somehow, Suzanne knew that was not what Claudia meant, so she just moved her head vaguely, neither agreeing or disagreeing. When Claudia laughed, Suzanne thought briefly of a boy she knew at St. Michael's. How far away was that? she wondered. He had liked her, taken her to his prom. Maybe he could help her now.

"I'm not talking about B&B's," Claudia said. "I mean pcilicibin mushrooms. Bo and I ate some and then went over to Tilden Park in Berkeley and looked out at the bridge and the bay and the hills. The sky is different in California. It's a high sky. Did you ever notice that?"

Suzanne shook her head. She had heard about people who took LSD and things like that. A boy back home who worked at the Esso station had taken something and gone crazy. One day he was pumping gas and he put the nozzle in someone's backseat, pouring gas all over the customer's new Volvo.

"That's the real bummer," Claudia said. "I was supposed to go to Berkeley. But my parents came to our apartment and dragged me out and shipped me off to this backwoods school so my grandparents can keep an eye on me."

"Maybe you can transfer in January?" Suzanne said hopefully.

Claudia shrugged. "Who knows? I'm here now. I'll just have to make the best of it."

Suzanne was the one who arrived first and took the bottom drawers and the bed near the radiator so her roommate wouldn't think she was selfish. She had a jewelry box that played "Lara's Theme" and a silver monogrammed brush and hand mirror.

After they all got to be friends, she discovered she was the only one who was still a virgin. But she lied and told them she had gone to third base once.

If she hadn't met them and become their friend, she would have married Ken Farrel, the president of Phi Sigma Kappa, who wanted to be a lawyer and move to Washington, D.C. She had started on that path. She got bids from three sororities and went to the Fall Frolic with Ken. But sometimes, wearing the multi-colored ribbons that signified she was a sorority pledge and walking with a group of other pledges, she would pass Claudia and Elizabeth. And it always seemed that they were doing something—no matter what it was—that was more important, and she would feel guilty; the double blue and gold ribbons on her sweater seemed like an emblem of her shallowness.

By the time the semester ended, she had met Abel and left the sorority. One day, as she was sitting with Claudia and Elizabeth, dressed in jeans and one of Abel's sweaters, Ken Farrel passed. "My God, Suzanne!" he said. "What's happened to you?"

But for a while back then, it was right. She stayed up late drinking wine with Claudia and Elizabeth and the three of them told each other all of their secrets. It was Suzanne who said to them one night that she had never before known what it was really like to have a friend, and now she had two. They had toasted to their friendship then, clinking glasses of cheap wine, crying and promising they would be this way forever.

Elizabeth was the one whose roommate never showed up and so she got to spend the entire year in a single. She taught them all to roll towels under the door so the smell of marijuana didn't spread into the hallway. On the first day of classes, Elizabeth walked into Freshman Lit 101 and fell in love with the T.A., a tall man with blue eyes named Howard Morgan. At first, he spent every weekend with her in the dorm. By the time the semester ended, he spent almost every night there.

Howard and Elizabeth had beliefs and causes right from the start. They didn't idly paint peace signs on the walls or say "oink" as the campus police walked by. Instead, they organized and protested and spoke in front of the student union. They went to Washington to march. They got thrown in jail. And they were so in love that Claudia and Suzanne may not have gotten to know Elizabeth at all if it weren't for the night the van of people from San Francisco arrived.

It was November, the Thursday night before a long weekend and most students had gone home early. But Suzanne didn't want to cut classes on Friday and Claudia wasn't expected at her grandparents' house until Saturday. So the two of them sat and watched TV and drank strong tea.

"This needs sugar," Suzanne said.

"Let's see if there's anyone left who has some. I'm going stir crazy anyway."

They walked down the hall, listening for music or laughter to indicate someone else was still around.

Elizabeth's door was wide open and she was sitting on the floor making a poster for an anti-Vietnam march in Boston. She was drinking red wine. Red wine in a time when women drank rum and Coke or a sloe gin fizz, or, maybe, a beer.

"What are you doing?" Claudia asked her.

"There's a war going on," Elizabeth said.

"Here? My God! And me out of my camouflage fatigues."

Suzanne cleared her throat uncomfortably.

"I think you're safe here," Elizabeth said.

"Good," Claudia said, and walked in the room.

Suzanne stayed in the doorway. It was rude to go into a room uninvited.

"We wanted to borrow some sugar," Suzanne explained. "For tea."

"We have a hot plate," Claudia said.

Suzanne shot her a dirty look, then said to Elizabeth, "You won't say anything, will you? You can have a cup of tea anytime you'd like."

Elizabeth smiled. She had a nice smile with large, even teeth. "I have a hot plate too. And I burn candles."

"I keep telling her everyone does but she can't believe so many people break the rules," Claudia said.

"Anyway," Elizabeth said, "I can't loan you any sugar because I don't use it. Or white flour. It makes you rot."

Suzanne's eyes widened. "Rot?"

"Animal fat too."

And then the noise began. First the horn honking. Then the shouting.

"They're calling Claudia," Elizabeth said.

The three women ran to the window. There was a van outside, painted in pink, black, and green psychedelic swirls.

"It's Bo!" Claudia shouted. "Come on!"

And they ran down the stairs and out the door, not even stopping to sign out. That was how it started. They took off into the night with Claudia's friends, who were driving around the country just to say hello to everyone they knew. After a while, Suzanne stopped saying that maybe they should go back and sign out properly. They drove a long way up the coast and slept on the beach, huddled together like kittens. The friends from California had hashish and they smoked it at dawn, then ran into the water, kicking up the sand, which glowed as if it were fluorescent, and fell at their feet like Roman candles.

CLAUDIA AND SUZANNE,
1966

Most of their conversations were like this, in the dark, Suzanne in her twin bed against the wall near the radiator, Claudia in her bed under the window. Even on cold winter nights she kept the window open wide while Suzanne huddled under a thick white comforter covered with fat yellow roses.

"I don't think my brother even likes women, if you know what I mean," Claudia was saying. "I mean, he never dates. Ever. He doesn't even look at women. Sometimes I kid him about it. I'll say, 'Ben, do you like boys or girls? Animal, vegetable, or mineral?' Are you listening to me, Suzanne?"

"Animal, vegetable, or mineral," Suzanne said without opening her eyes. Claudia talked more than anyone she'd known. She liked to close her eyes and drift off into near-sleep, Claudia's voice droning on like a comfortable lullaby.

"When I was in San Francisco last summer he'd take me to the Top of the Mark for drinks every other Friday.

He would always have two Manhattans. Always. I'd say, 'Come on, Ben, order a martini, just this once.' But of course he never would. That's what he's like. So exact. Kind of like you. In fact, now that I think of it, you and Ben are a lot alike. When we were kids I'd have to beg him to do anything. Climb a tree, go into town, anything. Ben would always worry if we really should, if it was all right. Like you. Do you see what I mean, Suzie?"

"Mmmm."

Claudia sat up, her threadbare secondhand quilt wrapped around her shoulders. Suzanne could smell mothballs from across the room.

"That thing smells," Suzanne mumbled. She pulled a strand of her hair across her face and sniffed in its clean, baby-shampoo smell, something she did to block out odors she found unpleasant—burning marijuana, incense, mothballs. She associated all of these smells with Claudia.

"When I was little," Claudia said, "I used to run away all the time. Really run, at full speed. Across the fields, down the road, all the way to town. My parents would have to come and find me and I'd cry the whole way home."

Suzanne opened her eyes. Claudia was looking out the window, her face tilted upward as if to absorb the moonlight.

"I could do it now," she said. "Run and run and run. Up the coast of Maine, all the way to Canada. Beyond Canada." The quilt had slipped off one shoulder. Her white skin seemed translucent against the blackness of the night. Suzanne thought that if she looked hard enough, Claudia's pale blue veins would be visible, even from the distance of the room, like the veins in fine marble.

"Are you unhappy?" Suzanne asked her. "Is that it?"

Claudia turned toward her.

"It's not a question of happy or unhappy. It's a restlessness. A need. Don't you have any needs, Suzanne?"

"Of course I do. Lots." But even saying that sounded fake to Suzanne. Needs? she thought. She had been raised to expect certain things—straight A's and boys who opened doors for her, monogrammed silver and delicate crystal that pinged when it was tapped. These other things that Claudia always talked about seemed foreign, alien to her. Yearnings. Achings. Suzanne shook her head.

"God," Claudia said suddenly, "I almost fainted when that guy read that essay about you in class today. It was like a poem. He compared you to an angel."

Suzanne felt herself turning red and was thankful for the darkness of the room. His voice had been deep as he read it. "I see her," Abel had recited, "a twinkle of diamond at each ear, wrapped in cashmere . . ." His eyes were turquoise, the color of the sea. They fixed on her as he spoke. Claudia had leaned over and scribbled on her notebook. It had taken all of Suzanne's strength to look away from him and down at what she'd written.

"Do you even know him?" Claudia asked her. She had gotten out of bed and loomed over Suzanne, her tangle of red hair falling forward so that Suzanne could feel its ends against her own.

"I've never even talked to him," she said.

"He's gorgeous."

"Gorgeous?" Suzanne laughed. "He's so scruffy-looking. Like a construction worker or something."

"You're crazy," Claudia shrieked. "He is the sexiest guy in that class. And I'm sure," she added in a teasing voice, "that he has a huge penis. He's just that type."

"Stop!"

"He does have one, you know."

"I don't care. I don't want to even think about him. He's not my type at all."

"What is your type? That guy with the shiny shoes and the crew cut? He looks like he works for the FBI."

Suzanne didn't answer. She closed her eyes again. Ken Farrel was her type. Like the boys back home. Lately it seemed like the whole world was going crazy, boys grew their hair long, everybody wore faded old dungarees. It was hard to find a boy like Ken amidst all of it. She tried to call his face to mind, but all she got was an image of Abel, with those incredible eyes.

"You don't even know your type," Claudia said, moving away from Suzanne.

Far off, down the long hallway outside their room, Suzanne heard the telephone ringing.

"You should talk," she said angrily. She was mad at Abel for intruding into her thoughts, mad at Claudia for making her question everything.

There was a knock on their door.

"Suzanne," a voice said. "Telephone."

"What time is it?" Suzanne said, pulling on her bathrobe and slippers. "It's after midnight, isn't it?"

"Probably Kenny boy got drunk at a fraternity party and he's out of his mind with lust for you," Claudia said.

Suzanne opened the door. Elizabeth from down the hall was standing there, wrapped in a short red kimono with pale blue birds on it.

"It's a guy," Elizabeth said.

Suzanne could smell marijuana in Elizabeth's hair. If someone had told her then that in a few weeks this woman would be her friend, she would never have believed it.

"It's after midnight," Suzanne said.

Elizabeth shrugged. When they reached her room, Howard opened the door.

"I missed you," he said, pulling her inside.

Suzanne walked past them without looking. It wasn't

94

right to have a guy in your room, especially after curfew. Especially for the entire night. She stepped into the telephone booth. There was an empty bottle of Coke inside. The phone receiver dangled from a stiff silver cord.

"Hello?" Suzanne said.

"Hi." The voice was deep, surprisingly male.

She knew it was Abel.

"Who is this?" she asked. Her mouth felt dry.

"Abel," he said. "From Lit 101."

"It's very late."

"Is it? I had no idea."

Suzanne pushed her fingers into each circle on the dial.

"I thought we could go for a beer or something."

"When?"

"Now."

"Now? Are you crazy?"

Claudia squeezed into the phone booth. "Who is it?" she mouthed. Suzanne tried to push her out. "Who?"

"Abel." Suzanne formed the name slowly.

"What room are you in?"

"It's after curfew," Suzanne said.

"Go. Go," Claudia mouthed.

"What room?" Abel said. "I can see in the freshman directory here that it's Weldin Hall. Right?"

Suzanne looked at Claudia. Her eyes were shining. "Go." She made a shooing motion with her hands. For some reason, Suzanne thought of Ken's red MG. Would you like the top up or down? he always asked her before she got in.

"I'm sorry," Suzanne said.

"How about tomorrow?"

"I don't think so. But thank you. And thank you for that lovely essay. It was very sweet."

"Are you nuts?" Claudia screamed as they walked back to their room.

"Quiet," a sleepy voice called out to them from behind a closed door.

Suzanne heard bed springs squeak rhythmically in Elizabeth's room.

"Are you nuts?" Claudia whispered fiercely.

"I'd be nuts to go out with him," Suzanne said. "Really nuts."

SUZANNE AND
ELIZABETH, 1966

"Let me see," Suzanne said to Elizabeth.

They were sitting on the floor in Suzanne's room. Elizabeth had cut a potato in half and carved a peace sign into its flesh. She rubbed it in ink, then stamped the impression onto grainy white paper, folded in half, with PEACE IN '67 written inside. She held a finished one up for Suzanne to see. Suzanne thought of the Christmas cards she'd sent, ornate Christmas trees flecked with gold sparkles, a shiny, fat star on top.

"Nice," she said.

Elizabeth laughed. "It's all right if you hate it."

"No," she said. "I hate mine."

"So," Elizabeth said, dipping the potato. "Are you taking Abel home for Christmas?"

"Are you crazy? My parents would die." She tried to picture Abel in her house, sitting by the stone fireplace, his army boots resting on one of her parents' pale Oriental rugs. "No way," she said.

"My parents are going to freak out when they meet

Howard. But I love him and if they make me choose—"
She shrugged.

Suzanne was fascinated by Elizabeth's sureness about everything. It seemed as if she were so much older than Suzanne, her voice confident, her actions certain. How do you know that Howard's the right one? she had asked her. I just know, Elizabeth told her.

More than anyone she'd ever known, Suzanne liked to talk to Elizabeth. After the first night she'd spent with Abel, she had gone straight to Elizabeth's room instead of to her own, still wearing one of his shirts, feeling bruised and sticky and dazed. She had told Elizabeth everything, the way his skin had felt, how she had moaned when his moustache brushed her thighs, what he had whispered to her. I have never felt so wonderful, Suzanne had said. Elizabeth had hugged her as if she were welcoming her to some private women's club.

"Where's Claudia, anyway?" Elizabeth asked. She blew on the card to make the ink dry faster.

"Skiing."

"She skis?"

"She met some guy at the Rathskellar last night. She drags me to all these places and then deserts me. Every time. She showed up here at about five o'clock this morning and brings this guy right into our room. I almost died. Can you imagine waking up with some strange guy with a ponytail standing over you. "We're going skiing," he said. "At Sugarloaf. Want to come?"

"What did you say?"

"No thank you. Their pupils were dilated like they'd taken God knows what."

Suzanne rolled out some wrapping paper with triangle-shaped gold trees. She measured the amount she needed carefully, cutting straight even lines. The first time Elizabeth had seen her, in the fall, carrying a yellow trunk up the stairs, she'd thought Suzanne looked like Sandra Dee. Sometimes she still thought so.

"There," Suzanne said, sticking a gold bow on top of the package.

"What's in there?"

Suzanne laughed. "Chanel No. 5. I give it to my mother every year and she gives it to me."

"How are you going to get all that stuff home?"

"Train."

"That's ridiculous. We'll drive you."

"Who?"

"Howard and me."

Suzanne looked up. She could never have her parents see Elizabeth and Howard. She was already worried about what they'd say when they saw her, with her hair unstyled, hanging straight down past her shoulders and wearing the used pea coat Abel had given her. They were going to ask her all about her friends and her dates and she had no idea what she was going to say.

"That's all right," she said. She pulled tightly on a ribbon wrapped around a long box with an umbrella for her father tucked inside. "I'm looking forward to the train ride. Really." She pulled tighter. The ribbon snapped, tearing unevenly in her hands.

"I won't hear of it," Elizabeth said. "Westchester's just a minor detour."

"It's way out of your way," Suzanne said, trying to think clearly. "To get to New Jersey you'll want to take the George Washington Bridge and—"

"It's no big deal," Elizabeth said.

The two women's eyes met.

"Great," Suzanne said, trying to sound cheerful.

"This is it."

Howard pulled into the driveway.

"There's no place like home," Elizabeth said.

Suzanne stared at the house. She felt like someone else lived there, someone she didn't even know. There was the house number, written in script over the door, and the evenly pruned hedges. But they looked only vaguely familiar, as if she'd seen them in someone else's photo album. She fingered the handle on one of her suitcases. Inside were all of her stuffed animals, a long-haired cat, a chubby bear, a droopy-eared lion. She felt an urge to hold them all on her lap.

She could still feel Abel inside her from that morning. Don't leave me, he'd whispered. Stay. We'll have our own Christmas right here. She had held him tight until he'd grown soft and slipped out of her.

"I feel so confused," Suzanne said. "Like I don't know who I am. I mean, I used to know."

"Do you want to drive around the block awhile?" Howard asked her.

"I feel like such a baby," Suzanne said.

"Are you feeling a little guilty?" Elizabeth said. "Do you think your parents will take one look at you and just know about you and Abel?"

"Sort of." Suzanne remembered how she had studied her image in Abel's mirror after they'd first made love to try to spot changes, signs that showed what she'd done. She thought of the things she'd whispered to him this morning in bed. I want you again. Again. Touch me here. She blushed thinking of this in the shadow of her parents' house. Suzanne focused on an image of the heavy silver tea service that sat on a polished table in the formal room of the sorority house she had joined briefly. Sisters in white gloves had handed her a cup of tea in bone china with a rosebud pattern.

"I'm all right," she said, taking a deep breath. She fumbled with the door handle, locking it accidentally then unlocking it and locking it again, unable to get the order correct. She tried to force Elizabeth's and Howard's images to blur in the front seat of his old Peugeot. But they didn't. Elizabeth's glossy black hair remained just so, Howard's patterned red kerchief seemed even more distinct. Finally, out of the car, in the fresh cold air, Suzanne stood with her bags and suitcases all around her. She ran her fingers through her hair, trying to make it take shape somehow.

The car jerked into reverse loudly.

"Wait," Suzanne said, grabbing at the car but not able to reach it.

Elizabeth opened the window.

"Would you like to come in for some eggnog?" Suzanne said.

Elizabeth smiled a gentle, knowing smile. Claudia had said she thought Elizabeth was a very old soul, you could see it in her eyes.

"Thanks," Elizabeth said. "But we should get going."

"Keep on trucking, huh?" Suzanne said, the words sounding artificial in the quiet suburban air.

"Yes. Right." Elizabeth smiled.

"Thanks," Suzanne said. "For the ride, I mean."

She turned and walked up the neatly shoveled drive. Her mother was in the doorway, with an apron over her frilly white blouse. The apron had silver bells embossed on the front, linked with holly. Suzanne walked, her thighs aching from clutching Abel to her, toward her house.

CLAUDIA AND
ELIZABETH, 1967

"Therefore," Claudia said, "I'm a typical Gemini."

Elizabeth looked over at her.

"I thought we were talking about astronomy. Like what's up there." She pointed to the sky.

"You say astronomy. I say astrology. Let's call the whole thing off."

Elizabeth kept her finger arched upward. The moon was a sliver in the inky blackness.

"Venus," she said. "Right there, under the moon. Mercury is to the right."

Claudia closed her eyes. She could smell rain in the air. She pulled at the grass beside the blanket they were laying on, dug her fingers into the earth. It felt cool and moist.

"You're going to fail that astronomy test," Elizabeth said. She poured some wine into a paper cup.

"I'm a history major. What do I need astronomy for anyway?"

"I always wanted to go there," Elizabeth said.

Claudia opened her eyes.

"Where?"

"The stars, the moon, the planets, the galaxies. Anywhere up there."

Claudia sat up and drank some wine right from the jug. It spilled down her chin and trickled onto her neck and blouse. She didn't wipe it off.

"Spring," she said, "and a young girl's thoughts turn away from science and toward love."

Elizabeth shook her head.

"I met a new guy," Claudia said. "He's so sexy. Rough and ready."

Elizabeth had heard Claudia describe so many men that it was hard for her to get excited anymore. In a few weeks it would be someone else. Someone gentle. Or brainy. Or exotic.

"He works on a farm outside of town," Claudia said. "He's not in school or anything. I dragged Suzanne down to hear banjo music last night and from the minute I laid eyes on him I had to meet him."

"What's his name?"

Claudia shivered, despite the warm spring air. She thought of the way he'd pushed into her last night, hard, the gravel in the parking lot digging into her knees, strains of the Cotton-eye Joe drifting from inside the bar, the zipper on his jacket hitting her as he moved from behind her.

"Hello," Elizabeth said.

"What?"

"Does he have a name?"

"Let's go get him," Claudia said, jumping up. "Let's go get him and go to the beach, swimming."

"What about astronomy?" Elizabeth said, but saying it, she was already gathering the blanket and books and charts, knowing that they would go.

"It's warm. It's spring," Claudia said. "That's all that matters."

At first, when he opened the door, Elizabeth wasn't sure he recognized Claudia at all. He just stood there, listening to her plan to go to the beach, then came outside and got into the car with them.

"I'm Elizabeth," Elizabeth said.

"Peter," he said. He was beautiful, his features chiseled, his mouth full. In one ear he wore a diamond stud. He didn't talk the whole way there.

"Tell him about Venus," Claudia said. "The brightest planet. Tell him about Mercury." Peter tipped the jug of wine back and swallowed. Elizabeth didn't say anything else.

As they walked down to the beach from the road, Claudia whispered to Elizabeth, "Real talkative, huh? The strong silent type." Then she broke into a run, shedding her clothes along the way to the water. At its edge she twirled around, then dove into a wave. Elizabeth looked up. Mercury was hidden now, covered by clouds. She stripped to her panties and followed Claudia.

"It's freezing," she said.

"It feels great," Claudia laughed. "Come on, Peter. It's wonderful."

On the shore, Peter began to undress, slowly. Elizabeth tried to look away, but couldn't. Under the water Claudia grabbed her hand. When he pulled his jeans off, he stood motionless for a moment and looked up toward the crescent moon. Elizabeth heard Claudia's breath catch. "He's like a god," she whispered, her voice sounding distant against the crashing waves, and very small. Elizabeth nodded. Their hands floated away from each other and Claudia swam toward Peter, her strong strokes cutting into the water like axes, chopping.

Elizabeth lay on her back, let the movement of the waves buoy her, keep her adrift. Through half-open eyes she saw her nipples, hard against the cold air, the foamy ocean water swirling around her stomach. She felt goosebumps on her arms. She heard Claudia laugh, water splash. Above her, Venus was a dim light behind the rolling clouds. It began to rain, so lightly at first that she wasn't sure if it was rain or spray.

In the distance, Claudia wrapped her legs around Peter. His mouth was cold and salty on hers. He supported her in his strong arms as the waves pushed against them. She could feel the current tugging her. When he entered her, she threw her head back, opened her mouth, and drank the rain.

SUZANNE, CLAUDIA,
AND ELIZABETH, 1967

"I saw *The Graduate* thirteen times," Claudia said. "I mean, I saw it at least twice a week, every week, for almost two months. And you know, it was hardly filmed in Berkeley at all. Just a few scenes were. Like when Benjamin's in that boardinghouse."

"What about those scenes on campus? When he's waiting for Elaine?" Elizabeth asked.

"No. That's actually Santa Cruz or someplace like that. God, I love that movie."

"Do you know what movie I love?" Suzanne said. "*Doctor Zhivago.*"

"I hated that movie," Claudia said. "All that snow. Trudge, trudge. Lara. Where are you, Lara? Trudge, trudge."

Elizabeth laughed. "I like the movie but not that stupid song."

"I love that song," Suzanne said. "My music box plays that song."

She hummed the song, stood, and waltzed with an

invisible partner, her peach-colored bathrobe opening slightly.

Elizabeth and Claudia applauded, poured more wine. They were in Suzanne and Claudia's room. It was May. The summer stretched before the three of them. They would all stay in Maine, even Suzanne, who'd had to be convinced. Only after she'd gotten a job at a bank in town could she justify staying.

She was going to live with Abel, in a little house by the beach. Just that afternoon Suzanne had shown it to them. It was white, with weather-beaten shingles and baby blue trim. They helped her make up a story for her parents. She would tell them she was living with Claudia still and use that phone number. Claudia would cover for her, get messages to her if they called. "It's so dishonest," Suzanne had said. "Look," Claudia had told her, "it will work out fine. What are friends for?"

"What a summer this will be," Suzanne said. She sat on the floor.

"You sexpot," Claudia laughed. "We've created a monster, Elizabeth."

"To summer," Elizabeth toasted.

"To us," Suzanne added.

"To us," Claudia said.

They drank their wine and poured more.

"How much of this stuff do we drink?" Elizabeth said, holding up the empty wine bottle.

"Not nearly enough," Suzanne said. "There's so much Chianti to drink, so little time."

"So much love to make, so little time, huh?" Claudia laughed.

"You've always been a sex-crazed woman, Claudia," Suzanne said. "I'm new at this. Do you want to know something? God. Too much wine to drink. Why did I ever start this?"

"What is this," Claudia said, "some deep dark secret?"

"No. I just mean you can't tell anyone."

"Who would we tell except each other?" Elizabeth laughed.

"I'm so embarrassed."

"What is it?" Claudia said.

"It's nothing really. It's just, sometimes when Abel and I, you know, do it, he stays inside me and—" She laughed, covering her face with her hands. "He recites me poetry. His poetry. I mean, it sounds so corny, but it is really so beautiful. He'd die if he ever knew I told you."

"I have a real secret," Claudia said. This is it, she thought. Saying it will make it truly real.

"A night for secrets," Elizabeth said.

"You guys are not going to believe mine," Claudia said. She swallowed hard. "I'm pregnant."

Suzanne's eyes opened wide.

"Oh, no," Elizabeth said. Her mind raced. "I know a doctor. In Boston."

Claudia shook her head. "I'm going to have it."

Suzanne's eyes widened more. "I'm sorry to ask this, Claudia. I mean, I have no right, but do you know who the father is?" Her voice was uneven.

"It's Peter. Peter from the farm."

"This doctor in Boston—"

"It was almost like I knew from the very moment it was conceived. I know that sounds crazy." For a moment, Claudia could smell the farm around her, hear the cows mooing softly, feel Peter's strong, sure movements. "It's an incredible thing. It feels wonderful and I just want to have it."

"What about school?" Suzanne asked her.

"I'm going to finish. I haven't thought everything out exactly, but I've always been pretty unconventional. Right? I mean, suppose he wants to get married or something. I don't know what I'll do about that. But I'll finish school. What's three more years?"

"He doesn't know yet?" Elizabeth said.

Claudia shook her head. She wanted to say that Peter seemed almost like a secondary part of all this, but she didn't.

"If you change your mind after you talk to him—" Elizabeth began.

"Thanks. You're both great for not telling me what to do and for not trying to talk me out of it."

"To tell you the truth," Suzanne said, "I want to talk you out of it. You're going to need money and a place to live. You don't just go and have a baby."

"Why not? Women do it all over the world. All the time."

"I know what you're like when you get an idea in your head," Suzanne said. "There's no talking you out of it."

There was a silence for a time, a comfortable silence. The women, without realizing it, moved closer together.

"Howard told me that if he ever had to go to Vietnam, he would run away to Canada," Elizabeth said suddenly.

"Wouldn't you want him to do that?" Claudia said.

"This is a secret. I mean, it's not the type of thing people talk about. It would have to be done so quietly."

"It isn't your secret. It's Howard's secret," Claudia said.

"No, it's mine. If he went to Canada, I don't know if I could go with him. It's running away."

"But he's in school. He's got a deferment," Suzanne said.

"He's starting that Ph.D. in New York this fall, but he's already anticipating that he may not stick with it. It's a real conservative department. But, the thing is, if he quits, he'll be eligible to go in the army."

"You would never leave Howard," Suzanne said. "You would have to go with him."

"I couldn't run away. He should be willing to go to prison for what he believes."

"Prison!" Suzanne said.

"This is Howard's decision," Claudia said. "Besides, he may like the school and it will all work out."

Elizabeth looked as if she might cry. "I don't know what I would do."

"When the time comes we'll be there," Suzanne said. "Even if you run off to New York and follow Howard to the wilds of Canada, we'll be there for you. You know that, don't you?"

Elizabeth nodded. "We just discussed it last night and it's been on my mind. Life without Howard would be—"

"Like life without us!" Suzanne laughed.

"All right, Suzanne," Claudia said. "Confess. What's your secret?"

"I already told you one."

"That doesn't count. That's a sex secret and I've told you a million of those," Claudia said.

"I want to move to a big city, like Boston, maybe, and get a fantastic job and make lots of money," Suzanne said.

"You horrible capitalist!" Elizabeth said.

"I'm afraid it's true."

"What about Abel?" Claudia asked.

"He'll come too. He'll teach writing. I'll buy him a tweed jacket and a pipe."

"That's not a secret."

"It is to Abel," Suzanne laughed.

"Let's sign our names in blood or something," Claudia said. "Like a pact."

"We don't need to do that," Suzanne said.

"That's right," Elizabeth said. "We're friends."

They smiled at each other. "Let's seal it in ice cream!" Claudia shouted.

And they piled into Abel's fluorescent green VW van and drove to the twenty-four-hour Howard Johnson's. There was only one waitress and the restaurant was full. Later, they argued over who got up and started taking orders first, Elizabeth or Claudia. They could agree that it wasn't Suzanne, who had to be convinced and then ended up getting the biggest tip, $3.00 from a man who said she was the only waitress in there that didn't look like some crazy hippie. "That's right," Elizabeth had told him, "she's a capitalist pig."

"We'll get lobsters," Suzanne said on their way home after she counted their tips. "We'll get lobsters and cook them at Abel's house. I mean, at Abel's and my house. We can cook them right on the beach and they'll be delicious."

SUZANNE, 1970

She could have sat in the Portland bus station for two hours to get a bus that required only one change, in Boston Or she could get on a bus right away and change three times—Boston, Providence, and New Haven.

"I want to leave now," Suzanne said to the ticket seller. He stood behind bars, like a man in a Monopoly jail.

"Honey, the later bus still gets to New York earlier. And that's with a two-hour wait! It's crazy to leave now."

Suzanne slipped the money through an opening at the bottom of the bars.

"Honey, listen, *three* bus changes. You could get lost. Or delayed and miss one of those connections. It happens, you know."

She pushed the money farther through the opening. The man shook his head, passed a ticket back through to her.

The thing was, she had to keep moving. If she sat there for two hours, she might cave in, lose control. This way, there was action, movement. She would get on the bus and keep moving toward New York. Getting off the bus and finding the next one was good. It would keep her mind on something else. Moving through the different bus stations, buying newspapers and gum and small bags of potato chips and cream soda for the ride, looking at the bums who crowded each station—it would all keep her busy. And in the end, she would be in New York and Elizabeth would be there waiting. Then she would collapse. But not until then.

Suzanne was afraid that the actual time on the buses would be the worst part of the trip. She thought Abel's presence might crowd her then, as New England sped by her. "Boston?" he had said. "Me in Boston with a wife and baby? Suzie, you know me better than that." Images did flicker through her mind, but they were made-up ones. Abel happy about the baby, asking when it was coming. Abel dressed in a tweed jacket and knit tie, kissing her good-bye as he went off to work. There she would be, radiantly pregnant, round and smiling, waving good-bye. That's what she thought of through Maine and New Hampshire. The other images, the true ones, did not surface.

Instead, she kept her mind moving. She read each city's newspaper from the front page to the funnies. Race riots in Boston schools. The Young Rascals play the Rhode Island Auditorium. The Red Sox beat the Yankees. And Charlie Brown struck out over and over at softball in each city. "Good Grief!" he moaned in the *Boston Globe* and the *Providence Journal*. She read through Massachusetts and Rhode Island and half of Connecticut.

When she changed buses in New Haven, afraid to be idle as the new one pulled away, she tried to do the crossword puzzles and word jumbles. The clues didn't make sense to her and she turned to her horoscope.

"Don't travel today. Watch out for domestic quarrels," one warned her. "Good day for travel," she read in another newspaper. "Harmony with loved ones."

Suzanne surprised herself by fantasizing about Ken Farrel, who was starting law school in the fall in Washington, D.C. She imagined them moving there together, to a town house in Georgetown. They would have a small backyard with a patio where they could have barbecues. She would get a couple of cats, long-haired gray ones that would sit on the windowsill and look out. In this fantasy there was no baby. There were two cats and fraternity brothers coming over for spaghetti dinners with their wives, and a silver Volvo, and Sunday brunches, where she and Ken would eat fluffy omelets filled with Gruyère and apples.

When the bus pulled into Port Authority, Suzanne was slightly confused. And then she saw Elizabeth waving to her, looking just pregnant enough to jolt her back into remembering what had happened and why she had come all this way. As soon as she saw Elizabeth, in a paint-spattered smock, her stomach jutting out slightly, her hair frizzy from the early summer humidity, Suzanne broke down.

The act of moving downtown toward Elizabeth's apartment soothed her somewhat. The subway station was hot and smelled of urine. A man stood in front of Elizabeth and rubbed his stomach suggestively. "Oooooh, Mama," he whispered through broken teeth. On the train, clutching swaying straps, Elizabeth kept asking her, "Are you okay?"

"No," Suzanne answered, over and over. "No."

Elizabeth guided her off the train, up the stairs, and through the streets. Suzanne tried to concentrate on her legs as they moved up and down on the pavement. She felt control seeping out of her like sweat. Tears fell on her

114

cheeks again, hot and fast. There was an old freight elevator up to the loft, and it squeaked and groaned as it moved them slowly upward. Suzanne began to whimper. Elizabeth pulled the heavy gates open and led Suzanne down a dark hallway and into the loft.

Inside, there was sunlight. It smelled of paint. Everywhere there were stretched canvases, some blank, others completed. Elizabeth brought Suzanne to a futon in a far corner and as soon as she sat, as soon as she stopped moving, Suzanne began to weep. Her crying was loud and hard. Her body shook. She felt Elizabeth's arm around her and collapsed against her body.

There had been no question of going to Claudia with this. When it had happened to her, Peter had done the noble thing. They had gotten married and moved to a little apartment over the garage at a friend's farm. It had seemed to Suzanne that Claudia, who was always wildly searching for something, had found it with Simon. She had another baby, Henry, almost right away. Claudia strapped them to her back and brought them everywhere—classes, hiking, even to Abel and Suzanne's, where they climbed on the furniture and pulled Abel's moustache.

How could she ever tell Claudia that Abel didn't want their baby? Didn't even really want her. Claudia would tell her to have it and the hell with Abel. "I would have had Simon on my own," she had said often enough. And then she would pick up her son and bask in his very existence.

But the fact was, she did marry Peter. She hadn't had to have Simon on her own. And she could go ahead with all her plans. In the fall they were moving the whole family to Amherst and she would go to graduate school in ancient Greek history. She talked about going to a Greek island for a year or so, to study. They would eat fresh fish from the sea and swim in the Aegean, and she and Peter would drink ouzo and maybe, she laughed, make more babies. What a wonderful place to make a baby, she said.

Suzanne wondered where this baby, her baby, had begun. She liked to think it was on a night on the beach, under the stars. There *had* been nights like that. And afterward, Abel would whisper love poetry to her, softly in her ear, brushing the sand from her hair as he spoke. If she did have the baby, that's the story she would tell it of its beginnings. The sand in her hair and the poetry and the love. How could she tell a child that its own father hadn't wanted it? Or her? No, this child's beginnings would have to be a secret. Suzanne would have to be silent, and the thought began a new wave of sobs. Howard brought tea and the night wore on.

The voices of the workmen from outside drifted upward.

"I'm opening this bag, and if it's a salami and provolone sandwich inside, I'm going back home and making my wife eat it."

The sun slowly filled the loft.

"That's it. I'm going all the way back to Sheepshead Bay and throwing this goddamn sandwich in her face."

Suzanne's eyes felt heavy. She sniffled, looked up.

The thought she had suddenly was of the baby as the only remnant of her and Abel's love.

She got up and walked over to the stove, where Elizabeth was making wholewheat pancakes. "I don't think I should have an abortion," she said.

Elizabeth turned to her. "I had one," she said. "In high school."

"Tell me about it," Suzanne said.

"I had this boyfriend in high school who looked like James Dean. At least to me he did."

Suzanne smiled, the first smile since she had arrived. Her head was beginning to clear.

"His mother worked nights and I'd go to his house while she was gone. We'd drink wine and make love. And then one night we went out to dinner, to Vallee's Steakhouse. It was right after I found out I was pregnant. We ordered all this food and drank martinis and hardly spoke at all. We had so little in common. I mean, there was no question about having the baby. At least not for me."

"He wanted it?"

"Well, I don't know if he really wanted it. He didn't want me to go away to school that fall. He tried to paint this wonderful picture of the life we could have together."

Suzanne nodded. She thought of the wonderful life she had described to Abel. "We're just too different," he had said. "All I want, Suzie, is to sit here and watch the tide come in and write some poems. That's all."

"He told me a story," Elizabeth said. "A Chinese legend about lovers being separated. These two lovers were exiled to different galaxies and were heartbroken. But once a year they were reunited by crossing a bridge in the sky made completely of sparrows."

"What an image," Suzanne said. "Two lovers crossing a bridge of sparrows after being separated for a year. It's beautiful."

"It's the Milky Way, really. Connecting galaxies."

Not even the Milky Way could connect Abel and me again, Suzanne thought.

"He wants to sit on the beach and watch the ocean," she said.

"What do you want?" Elizabeth asked softly.

"To go to business school. I could get such a great job afterward, with an MBA. I could have a very good life."

117

If she didn't have the baby, Suzanne thought, she could start a new life in Boston. Forget Abel altogether. "Everyone has one true love," he had told her. "And you are mine." The thought of not having the baby, of erasing Abel from her life, sent a sharp pain through her. Suzanne imagined those first months of school, when she had made all her choices. They all seemed wrong now. She thought of walking past Claudia and Elizabeth and feeling drawn to them, pulled in a different direction. She had done it all wrong.

Maybe, she thought, this baby is a girl and I can show her all the right choices, be sure she makes them. She could start now by making her own right choices. She could put the past behind her, not dwell on her mistakes. But she would have the baby as a reminder, always, of where she had been.

Suzanne stood shakily. "I . . . I have to go."

"Go?" Elizabeth said.

"I want to go to Boston. I have so much to do."

And even as Elizabeth directed her out, bewildered, Suzanne was looking beyond her. This time, she took a direct train to Boston. Suzanne walked out of South Station and hailed a cab. The first thing she would do, she decided, after checking into a hotel room, was to get a haircut. She wrapped a strand around her finger tightly, remembered Abel's large hands in her hair, brushing off sand, then froze the image like a snapshot, and stored it away.

ELIZABETH, 1972

Saskatchewan. Alberta. Nova Scotia. The names jumped at them from the map. Howard's finger traced the shape of Canada.

"Saskatchewan," Elizabeth said.

From their apartment, they heard trucks pull in and out of the warehouse below them. The workmen shouted to each other. In the distance, a siren sounded.

"Ottawa," Elizabeth said.

She bounced Rebekah on her knee. The baby's mouth was always turned down, as if she were constantly on the verge of tears.

"I never thought we'd get such a cranky baby," Elizabeth said as Rebekah squirmed.

"Maybe we got the wrong one," Howard smiled.

Elizabeth thought she could live in that smile, crawl into it and shape herself against it. And his eyes. Howard's eyes were so blue that strangers sometimes stopped him and told him he had the most beautiful eyes they'd ever seen.

Rebekah twisted her body uncomfortably. She disliked being held, but when they put her down she screamed until she was picked up again. At night she sometimes whimpered even as she slept, her hands clenched into tiny fists. Elizabeth had been sure they would have a boy, a gentle baby with Howard's smile. This baby had been born scowling. She had lots of thick black hair that stood around her head like a permanent that went wrong. Already there were creases between her eyes from frowning.

"Do you want to take her back? Exchange her for a different model?" Howard said.

"No," Elizabeth said, "let's keep her. I understand I wasn't such a lovable baby either. Colicky."

Howard took the baby in his arms.

"Hello, Rebekah," he said. "What's the matter there, kiddo?"

Rebekah's face relaxed a little. All of her smiles were saved for her father.

Elizabeth picked up the map and looked at Howard.

"You think it's running away, don't you?" he said.

Rebekah pulled at his chin.

"Don't you?" Elizabeth asked.

"I'm not married to Joan Baez," he said. "No one will take notice if I go to prison."

"I'll notice. And someday this cantankerous kid of ours will grow up and she'll notice. She'll know we didn't run away."

Rebekah wrapped her fingers in Howard's hair. Sometimes Elizabeth would find them asleep like that, the baby's fingers clutching her father's hair.

"There is, of course—" he began.

"Another option."

"Going."

"A C.O."

"That is what I am," he said. "A conscientious objector."

"You could go and shuffle papers somewhere."

"That's why I left graduate school. I didn't want to shuffle any more papers."

"How about mopping floors in a hospital?" Elizabeth looked at the map. Bay of Fundy.

"I talked to Bob. From the deli. You know who I mean?"

Elizabeth nodded, pictured the man who filled hero sandwiches with tuna salad or corned beef, his long hair held back by a powder blue hairnet.

"They put him in Special Services. He speaks Thai. His mother's from Thailand and he lived there for a while. They sent him to learn Vietnamese and he went over as an interpreter. He never had to fight."

They looked at each other. Rebekah whimpered as she fell asleep, tightened her grip on Howard's hair.

"He told me that he feels he helped get peace in a peaceful way."

"You speak Japanese," Elizabeth said.

Howard smiled.

Oh, please, Elizabeth thought, let me climb into that smile and stay there forever.

"Do you remember," Howard said, knowing that of course she remembered, "what I told you on our very first date?"

Beer and pizza at the local college hangout. I've never seen such gorgeous eyes, she had said. Pizza with olives and mushrooms, the same combination they got now at Arturo's on Houston Street.

"I spent six months in Japan," Howard had said that night, "learning the language and the philosophy. I was in a motorcycle accident when I got back and on the admittance form I listed my religion as Buddhist. They thought I was being sassy." He had laughed then. "I'm probably the only guy who took his language requirement for grad school in Japanese."

"You told me to eat quickly because you wanted to take me home and kiss every inch of my body," Elizabeth said.

"I believe I was true to my word."

"If you go as a C.O. and they put you in Special Services like they did with Bob from the deli—"

"He said he felt like he helped achieve peace in a peaceful way. And through the system."

"Will you come back in one piece?"

"How could I not come back?" Howard said softly.

He disentangled Rebekah's fingers from his hair. As soon as her fingers were free, she grabbed Howard's forefinger and held on tight. Elizabeth wanted to grab his hand, too, and hold it so tightly he wouldn't be able to leave unless he took her with him.

"Some grip," Howard said.

Don't let go, Elizabeth thought.

Howard wiggled his finger free from his daughter's grip, and gently laid her in her crib.

Life without Howard was the hardest thing Elizabeth had known. Rebekah cried through the night. New York City never had a hotter summer. During the day, an old pea green fan spit choppy hot air at Elizabeth as she painted. She was having her second show in the fall and, as she planned for it, memories of her first show that spring flooded her. Sometimes she had to put down her brushes until the images passed.

She had tie-dyed Rebekah's outfit for the opening that spring, purple and pink broken circles intersecting, bleeding into each other. Howard had stood beside her, so proud that his eyes shone stronger and bluer than ever before. Later, Howard had told her that she had upstaged her own paintings, that was how beautiful she looked. They laughed at the man who showed up in a paisley print Nehru jacket with a fat white rabbit on a leash. When it was all over, they took champagne to the roof and drank to her success. And to their love. The city blinked at them.

Since he'd been gone, he wrote to her every day. She read the letters over and over, silently to herself and then out loud to Rebekah as she wailed into the sticky night.

At six o'clock every night, Elizabeth sat in front of the TV, an old Zenith that elongated all the images on the screen. Helicopters whirred, their rotors distorted so they looked like lava lamps, dripping into the jungle behind them. She scanned the pictures for a glimpse of Howard, even though she knew he was somewhere beyond all that, in a hot hut, where the war played in the background like a distant transistor radio. At eleven o'clock she looked again.

Elizabeth wrote to Claudia. "We want Rebekah to grow up free."

"We're looking for a farm," Claudia wrote back. "Maybe we can all live there together. You can teach the boys about the constellations. All I can tell them is they're both Libras."

It was winter when he came back. The very end of winter. March. A day so cold that even in the apartment puffs of air came out of her mouth when Elizabeth spoke. She dressed Rebekah in layers of clothing, Elizabeth's own knee socks over the child's legs, the bright zigzags of yellow, pink, red, and purple climbing toward her hips.

Elizabeth decided to make vegetable chili. She sat Rebekah on the countertop as she chopped eggplants, tomatoes, and squash. The chopping helped to keep her hands warm. Every now and then the radiator hissed.

Elizabeth had placed a bowl of orange peels and cinnamon sticks on top of it and the steamy air smelled vaguely spicy.

Rebekah pointed to the bowls of vegetables. "Yuck," she said.

"Not yuck, Rebekah. Yum."

"Yuck."

The elevator door slammed downstairs. The gates pulled shut.

"Sounds like we have company. Maybe Mrs. Santini has brought us some more soup."

Since Howard had left, Elizabeth and Rebekah had often eaten dinner with different families in the neighborhood. They were proud that Howard had gone off to war even though Elizabeth made a point of telling them that he was a conscientious objector. "He doesn't fight," she told them. "He translates messages." Still, grandfathers showed her their World War I uniforms and their wives brought out sepia-toned photographs of proud sons in World War II.

"Soup," Rebekah said. "Yuck."

"No, kiddo. That's another yum."

Often, Mrs. Santini brought them thick escarole soup, full of chopped eggs and celery and carrots. "Usually," she had told Elizabeth, "I put in little tiny meatballs, as little as this. But for you, I leave them out. Even though babies need meat to grow."

"Can you say escarole?"

"No," Rebekah said.

The elevator grunted and groaned toward them.

"Can you try?"

"No."

"Try, Rebekah. Come on. Es—ca—role."

"No!" she wailed. Her face crumpled, turned red.

Elizabeth heard the elevator gates slide heavily open.

"Come on. Don't cry now. Mrs. Santini's here. Don't cry."

Rebekah cried louder.

Elizabeth scooped her up and carried her to the door. A knock.

"Mrs. Santini," Elizabeth said as she opened it.

Rebekah pounded on her mother's shoulders.

"It's good to know," Howard said, "that nothing has changed."

He had lost weight. His hair had thinned. He had a thick short beard crowded with gray hairs. Howard drew them into his arms and underneath the smell of days of travel, Elizabeth smelled him. She buried her face in his chest and breathed him in. Already Rebekah had found his beard and clutched it as her cries faded.

"You can't just quit the army," Elizabeth said.

"I did."

"How? Did you write a formal letter of resignation? Fight with the boss?"

They were in bed, under three quilts in the darkness. Elizabeth had lit fat candles, white ones, that sent round chubby shadows onto the ceiling. Rebekah snored loudly in her crib. They drank hastily chilled champagne, left over from her fall show.

She felt giddy. From the champagne and from Howard.

"I just quit. Stopped working."

"What did you do all day?"

"Walked around mostly. Meditated."

Elizabeth remembered them driving to Boston back in college to listen to the Maharishi Mahesh Yogi. He lectured about transcendental meditation. TM, everyone called it. Howard hadn't liked the little man in white with the flowing beard. She had. There was a simplicity about him, a kind of peace. "Oh, no," Howard had groaned,

125

"you'll go off to India with the Beatles. Learn sitar music. Marry Donovan." She had tried it for a while, repeating her mantra over and over each morning.

"Did you dredge up your old mantra?" Elizabeth said, clutching Howard's hand under the quilts.

Howard laughed. "Funny you should ask. I ran into Paul McCartney in the jungle. He sends his love."

Howard had found his peace. That was apparent to Elizabeth. She had found hers when she met Howard. And that balanced with the joy she felt each time she picked up a paintbrush. Life, they both thought, was all about balance, a perfect circle with all the parts equal and full.

"It was all wrong to be there," Howard said softly. "Bob from the deli may have felt he was doing something peaceful, but I didn't. It was all war. That's it."

In their months apart, life had become clearer to them. They both knew that living a pure life and not supporting the war in any way was the only answer for them.

Howard had decided to apply to a program in Japan to learn to be a potter. Elizabeth could paint the patterns for him. It was the perfect way to combine philosophy and art and lifestyle. It was a way to keep their circle balanced. And that night, sipping champagne together in the dark, part of the answer was in Claudia's letter. "I found it," she wrote, "a big old farm that, with a lot of work, can support us all. At least come and see it. There's a barn and grass and a pond in the back—perfect for the kids. Perfect for us all."

"We should go to see it," Elizabeth said.

"A farm," Howard said.

"Maybe the country life will make Rebekah smile."

"Don't expect miracles," Howard laughed.

"Why not? You're back, aren't you?"

"Small miracle."

Elizabeth put her hand on Howard's chest. If the room weren't so dark, she would have seen gray hairs there.

"By the way," Howard whispered later, "this dishonorable discharge means I can never work for IBM."

"That's okay," Elizabeth whispered back, "I won't tell Suzanne."

They drove to the farm on the first Saturday in April. As soon as they saw it, they both knew it was right. A crooked crab apple tree was in bloom, its tiny flowers so delicate that Elizabeth could never quite capture them on canvas, though she tried for years later. Already, Claudia's sons had filled the yard with children's things. Scooters and trucks and blocks.

Howard picked up a spongy yellow ball.

"A Nerf ball," Claudia told him. "For Nerf baseball."

"Maybe I should stick to Frisbee."

"Come on," Claudia laughed, her red hair shining like a polished penny in the sunlight, "you've got to keep up with the times."

All around them there was the quiet noise of the country—birds and crickets, someone sawing in the distance.

Simon came over the hill from the pond, wet and tanned, wearing only a pair of faded cut-off jeans with long strings dangling from the bottom. "Here," he said, and handed Rebekah a small bouquet of wild daisies. "These are for you."

She looked up at him and broke into a wide smile.

"That's it," Elizabeth said. "If he can charm Rebekah, he can charm anyone."

"He charms me every day," Claudia said.

"Maybe we'll be in-laws someday," Howard laughed.

"Let's move in first," Elizabeth said, "and then wait twenty or thirty years."

They all watched as Rebekah let Simon take her hand and lead her up the hill.

SUZANNE, 1972

The real estate agent looked like Suzanne's old Barbie doll—frosted blond hair in a bubble cut, pointed breasts, and tiny feet in spike heels.

"I think, honestly, you'd be better off in Newton. Or Wellesley." The woman's dark green eyes looked down at Sparrow. "I mean, the only thing you could afford, or rather, in your price range, is in an unsavory neighborhood."

She leaned across her desk and pointed to a spot on the map she had opened in front of Suzanne.

"Like here."

Suzanne didn't look at the map.

"I think," she said in a controlled voice, "that the South End is going to turn around. It will be an excellent place to invest in property right now. That's what I do for a living. Investments, Miss Wills." Suzanne could not bring herself to call the woman "Candy," as she had requested.

"Please," the realtor said again, "Candy."

"Perhaps there's someone else here who would be willing to show me the property I'm interested in."

"I'm willing to show it to you," she said quickly. The woman smiled. Her lipstick was coral. "I just want you to understand what the neighborhood is like. That's all, Suzie—"

"Don't call me that." A flash. Abel caressing her hair, wrapping it around his fingers, whispering "Suzie."

"I'm sorry. Suzanne. Mrs.—"

"Why don't you just show me the town house on St. Botolph Street?"

Miss Wills unfolded a second map, this one of the MBTA subway system.

"You would have to use the Symphony stop on the T," she said, pointing with her pencil and shaking her head. Her fingernails were perfectly shaped coral ovals. "Not a real safe stop. I mean, an attractive woman, alone, with a two-year-old child." She shook her head again.

Suzanne could imagine Miss Wills—Candy—in Barbie's black chiffon cocktail dress with the tight bodice and full skirt made of layers and layers of scratchy material.

Miss Wills sighed. "All right," she said. "Maybe once you've looked at it you'll see what I mean."

Suzanne felt, more and more, the importance of planning. And Miss Wills could never understand how this property on St. Botolph Street fit into the plan. All through graduate school, cramped with Sparrow in a studio apartment in Brighton, Suzanne had taken the subway and walked all over the city studying the neighborhoods. She watched them rebuild warehouses in the North End and panicked because she hadn't saved enough money to invest there while the prices were still low. Finally, out of school and with money for a down payment, she had walked around the South End, where old town houses crumbled and signs that read FOR SALE OR RENT were springing up everywhere.

Letters from Claudia and Elizabeth talked about them looking for a farm. They wrote about space and trees and fresh air. Reading the letters, Suzanne longed for the comfort of their friendship. She longed for the little house in Maine that was drafty with the ocean air. But after she read each letter, Suzanne tore it into tiny perfect squares. Sometimes, especially alone at night on the lumpy sofabed she slept on, she imagined them there with her. Somehow, they would manage to make her laugh. "The Queen of Weldin Hall in this dump," Claudia would probably say if she ever saw the small apartment.

But to Suzanne, Claudia and Elizabeth were living symbols of her mistake. And she had sworn to leave the past behind her and start over. In a way, she paid for her mistake every day. She had taken on so much alone. And she had to make it all work, to come out right. Her old friends would reminisce, talk about Abel. They would show her pictures of their families, strong husbands, and children. It was too much for her. If ever she had to see them again, let them into her life for even a little while, Suzanne would show them how well it had all turned out. Otherwise, she would never be able to live with herself. It would be like advertising her mistake, making it permanent somehow. No. Someday, perhaps, they would see her as an accomplished career woman with a beautiful daughter who had turned out just right.

The management training program at the investment firm was the first step for her. Only the top five trainees would be offered positions at the end of the six months. And only the best of those five would move up in the firm. Suzanne was going to be one of them. And she planned to move up rapidly.

"Here we are," Miss Wills said.

She parked her yellow Datsun but didn't get out. The sidewalk was crowded with people on plastic and metal lawn chairs. Radios blared. Old men in sleeveless T-shirts and women in housedresses sat in front of the old brownstones that lined the streets. A pit bull puppy on a chain sniffed at the car. The air smelled garlicky.

"A lot of Puerto Ricans," Miss Wills said, tapping her coral fingernails on the steering wheel.

Suzanne got out of the car and lifted Sparrow onto the sidewalk.

"Hey, lady," a toothless man said, "you lost?"

"May I have the keys to the apartment, please?" Suzanne said. She stuck her hand in through the car window. The puppy sniffed at her and wagged its tail. "You can wait in the car if you'd like."

"No. No, I'll come in with you."

They walked down the block and into one of the old buildings. As they entered, Suzanne halted right inside the doorway. She heard a buzz saw from across the street. She turned and looked out. The building there was being renovated. She smiled as she followed Miss Wills into the apartment. The ceilings inside were high, the rooms long and narrow. Suzanne could smell roach spray.

"A real fix-it-up," she said. Already in her mind she was stripping the linoleum off the floor and replacing the torn and spotted wallpaper.

"It needs more than a little face-lift," Miss Wills said. She pointed to the staircase. A broken banister showed splintered wooden spokes all the way to the top.

Suzanne removed a broken shade from the front window and sunlight streamed in. The brightness made the apartment seem even more faded and dingy. From outside, salsa music drifted in. She watched the workmen across the street, armed with ladders and buckets of paint.

"I'll take it," she said.

132

"What?"

Suzanne turned. Across the room was a fireplace that had been boarded up, the mantel painted a heavy green.

"I said I'll take it."

She scooped Sparrow into her arms and walked out.

After all this was over, Suzanne promised herself a manicure. Her fingernails had all broken, her hands were full of scabs and fresh cuts and bruises. She had never hammered anything but a picture into a wall before this. She had never wallpapered, or sanded, or even cleaned so much. Sometimes at night she was so tired from her job that she wanted to just come home and fall into bed. But she never did. She picked up Sparrow at day care, made them dinner, then worked on the apartment. More than once she had fallen asleep on the floor, surrounded by tools and wallpaper samples.

Suzanne looked away from her hands and poured herself another glass of wine. She had discovered hardwood floors under the layers of roach-encrusted linoleum in the living room. Her back ached from nights of scraping it off on her hands and knees so she could sand the floor underneath.

Exhausted, she leaned her head against the wall. My next apartment, she thought, will be new and clean. No one will have ever used the toilet. The shower will work. The oven will light without any trouble.

Suzanne closed her eyes and imagined the farm where Claudia and Elizabeth had moved. She pictured the crab apple tree, the pond, the hill covered with daisies. What would they say if they saw this place? she thought, looking around. Elizabeth would probably roll up her sleeves and start helping. She would know how to steam off old wallpaper and how to use the sander. She would know the difference between a chisel and pliers. Somehow, Elizabeth always seemed to know everything.

Sometimes, Suzanne blamed them for her situation. But she knew she was wrong to feel that way. It was all her doing. That time with Abel, with them. Thinking of it, she shook her head, as if to make it all go away. She had to make up for what she'd done. She had to do it on her own. Even her parents had made that clear. They had never acknowledged Sparrow. Last Christmas, in a burst of loneliness, Suzanne had sent them a cheery letter and a package with a small bottle of Chanel No. 5 and a box of Belgian chocolates. They sent her an elaborate card with silver snowflakes embossed on the front and their names engraved on the inside, the same card her father sent his clients.

Again, Abel's face floated in front of her. There would be another man someday, when she was settled. Maybe he wouldn't make her feel the way Abel had, but he would be more like her. And that's what she needed. She would give their—no, her daughter a good life.

And then, feeling exhausted down through her bones, Suzanne cried. She cried for Abel, and for her old friends, and for the mistakes she had made that would not go away unless she made them go away. She cried because she hadn't had the time to read Sparrow a bedtime story. Suzanne reached down. Her tears fell onto the sticky wooden floor she had uncovered as she pulled out one more crumbling square of linoleum.

"Mommy," Sparrow said.

Suzanne dipped the roller into the pan of paint. The color that had seemed to be a soft pink on the sample chart had turned the walls in the upstairs hallway the color of Pepto-Bismol. One more coat, she thought, repeating it like a mantra to herself as she painted white over the other paint. One more coat.

It was a Sunday, rainy and hot. Sparrow sat on the new window seat with a picture book.

"Mommy," she said again. "Look. Boys."

"Sparrow, there are no boys in that book. Those are all farm animals."

"No. Outside."

Suzanne put the roller down and looked at the wall. It still looked very pink.

"Mommy."

The hall window looked down on the street. Sparrow was on her knees gazing out. Last night, when they had come in from the supermarket, the street had been littered with pigs' feet. Dozens of them had spilled from a truck. What are they? Sparrow had asked in horror. Suzanne hadn't answered. Now she watched out the window as the rain sent them racing down the street.

"See." Sparrow pointed.

"Don't touch the glass," Suzanne said, grabbing the little girl's finger. "You'll make marks."

Down below them, on the sidewalk, were two little boys in bright yellow rain slickers running beside the steady stream of pigs' feet. Suzanne heard them laughing and a woman shriek, "They're feet! I swear they're feet!"

The woman came into view then. She wore a lime green rain slicker. The color of Abel's old van, Suzanne thought, and frowned. Now, why would she make that association? She gasped. The woman was Claudia. She saw that now. The long skinny legs, the loud laugh, the bright red tendrils sticking out from the hood of the raincoat.

"Oh, no," Suzanne said. Her heart raced. "Get away from the window," she said, and grabbed Sparrow. In a low crouch she led her to the stairway.

Sparrow giggled. "Is this a game?"

"Shhhh."

"Mommy—"

The doorbell rang.

How could she come here? Suzanne thought. She covered Sparrow's mouth with her hand. If only it was different. If only she could let her in, make Bloody Marys and French toast. If only she weren't so embarrassed. Go away, she thought. Let me live my life with all of you out of it.

The doorbell rang again.

"Is anyone home?" Claudia shouted. "It's raining pigs' feet out here."

"Mommy," Sparrow said, twisting her head free.

Suzanne shook her head.

She heard them as they walked away. Suzanne sighed, stared down the new banister to the front door. She could still smell varnish.

"Is this a game?" Sparrow laughed.

"I wish it were," she said.

She and Sparrow walked back to the window. In the street, Claudia led her sons twirling right through the puddles. Their voices were clear. "What a glorious feeling," they sang. "We're happy again."

S U Z A N N E ,   1 9 7 3

Suzanne knew every room of that little house in Maine. Every crack in the wood. The way the wind whistled through the kitchen windows. She had hung wind chimes on the back porch—long silver ones, made from seashells and two pieces of copper. In a strong breeze the curtain actually blew about. Abel never got around to caulking the windows.

He had never seen Sparrow. When she was born, Suzanne had written him a note, telling him that old Chinese legend Elizabeth had told her in New York that time. Had she hoped then that Sparrow would reunite her to Abel? He sent her roses. An extravagance, she knew. They were white, with a blush of peach in their petals.

Once, when Claudia and Peter were visiting friends, they spotted Abel as he walked out of the bookstore in town. He hadn't asked about her until the very end, as they started to walk away. How's Suzie? he had said. He seemed desperate, Claudia had written.

It was winter. No snow, but gray skies and bitter cold. Already the radio played Christmas carols. The little house was right across the street from the ocean. The water was as dark and gray as the sky.

"It's going to be very cold," Suzanne said to Sparrow as they got out of the car.

"Where are we?"

Suzanne looked across the street. She recalled the inside of that house, the sloping ceiling in the bedroom. The tiny floral pattern on the wallpaper in the living room. The yellow and green squares on the kitchen floor.

"Where?" Sparrow said.

Suzanne looked down at her daughter. Not even four yet and already questioning everything. What would she be like at ten? At fifteen?

"Maine."

"Where's Maine?"

"Please, Sparrow."

"Is that the ocean?"

She should have called. Suzanne looked back across the street. She had to see him and prove that things were better this way. Her career, finally leaving behind the apartment on St. Botolph Street and buying the new one on the waterfront. It was all falling into place. Now all she had to do was see Abel and settle it finally. She would feel better seeing that he was right where she'd left him.

"Are we swimming?" Sparrow asked her. "I don't have a swimming suit."

"We're visiting."

They crossed the street. Suzanne felt butterflies in her stomach. Maybe he'll change his mind, she thought for an instant. He'll see us and change his mind.

"No," she said out loud.

"No what?"

Suzanne shook her head.

The doorbell was broken. Suzanne knocked, then, when there was no answer, she peeked in the living room window. A Christmas tree sparkled with silver tinsel and tiny white lights.

"Are those snowflakes on that tree?" Sparrow asked.

"No one's home," Suzanne said.

"Why don't they melt?"

"They're magic snowflakes," a voice behind them said.

It was Abel, his arms full of firewood.

"They're lights, Sparrow," Suzanne said. "Just lights."

They followed him inside. Nothing had changed. It still felt the same, smelled the same. Suzanne and Sparrow sat on the old couch. Suzanne traced the pattern on the spread that covered it. They had bought it together, she remembered.

"I'm thirsty," Sparrow whispered.

Suzanne watched Abel's back as he placed the firewood in the storage bin by the fireplace. She thought of the fine blond hair on his shoulders.

He stood and faced them, wiping his hands on his jeans.

"Well," he said.

"We were just passing through," Suzanne said.

He nodded.

"I'm doing very well," Suzanne blurted out.

Abel smiled. "I'm sure you are, Suzie," he said.

"Yes."

They looked at each other. Come back with me, she thought.

"Boston," she said, "is lovely. We just moved to a new apartment. It's very large, too large for the two of us, really. It overlooks the harbor."

"Still a sucker for those ocean views, huh?"

She thought about the nights they'd spend on the beach watching the way the moonlight hit the ocean.

"I own it actually," she said, forcing herself to concentrate on the apartment, on things that were real.

"The ocean?" Abel laughed. "You are doing well."

Suzanne didn't laugh. She felt as if she were unraveling. She felt weak. Was it from the sound of his voice? She took a deep breath. "It has three bathrooms," she said.

Sparrow got off the couch and walked over to the Christmas tree. She still had her coat on, all buttoned up. And her woolly pink mittens.

"One bathroom," Suzanne continued, "is all black. In a certain light it looks almost purple. So I got lavender blinds and towels and soap to pick up that hint of violet."

Abel looked at her, puzzled.

Why am I talking about bathrooms? Suzanne thought.

"May I please take them off?" Sparrow asked, and held up her mittened hands.

Suzanne nodded.

"The view is incredible," she said.

"Had you really forgotten it?"

"I mean my view. From the apartment."

"So you are a city girl after all," Abel said.

Suzanne bit her lower lip.

"And you?" she asked.

"We made our choices a long time ago," he said without looking at her. "I belong here."

"Choices can't be unmade?" she said.

"Please," Abel said softly. "Don't."

She stood up.

"Sometimes," he said, "I take a poetry writing workshop at the college."

He walked over to her.

"In the morning," he said, "I run along the beach. You know, the ocean never looks the same. The color, the sound, even the smell, it's always different. I make money doing construction work here and there. Last spring I worked on the new mall. Of course, there's not much work this time of year. And at night I like to have some Jameson's and work on my poems."

Suzanne nodded.

"I don't know why in the world we came," she said. Her voice shook.

"You are still," he said, "so beautiful."

They were standing as close as two people can without actually touching. She could hear him breathe, as if he were beside her in bed, his head buried in her hair.

"Sparrow," Suzanne said, as if the word could break a spell.

The little girl reached out and touched one of the tiny white lights.

"Mommy," she said, "these snowflakes are hot."

SUZANNE, CLAUDIA, AND ELIZABETH, 1973

T he apartment still smelled new. In the month since Suzanne had sold the St. Botolph Street apartment, and moved into this new high-rise overlooking the harbor, she had relished the smells of fresh paint and varnished floors and plastered ceilings all done by someone else. The kitchen appliances were still shiny. She was the first person to ever fill the refrigerator or use the dishwasher. She got a thrill from running her fingers over the smooth, clean surfaces of the stove and countertops.

Suzanne stood in the doorway of the kitchen and inhaled. The Swiss chocolate and fresh vegetables mixed with the smells of newness from the apartment itself.

"Mommy," Sparrow said. The little girl sat on a white wooden stool in the center of the kitchen. Her legs moved back and forth against the rungs. "Why is there so much food? Are we having a feast?"

"Sparrow," Suzanne said, "don't kick the stool like that." She began to silently organize her preparations for the luncheon.

"Stool?" Sparrow said. She stopped moving her legs.

"That's what you're sitting on. A stool."

"It is?"

"Yes. What did you think?"

"I thought it was a chair."

Suzanne was going to make bisque from scratch. She brought the lobsters home, their claws held together with tiny green rubber bands, squirming in the bag. Sparrow thought they were pets. She had been denied kittens, goldfish, and hamsters for all her three years and thought that at last her wish had come true.

The lobsters were on the kitchen counter. A large pot of water was on the stove.

"What are their names?" Sparrow asked.

"They don't have names," her mother said.

Suzanne was ready to begin. Cookbooks were opened to the recipes she was using. A list of ingredients, first carefully prepared, then, with each item carefully crossed off, had been double-checked. Someday, she thought, she would have things like this catered, everything done for her as she sat in the living room and had cocktails with her guests. But now, while her job was still new and her income not yet where she wanted it, she would have to do it all herself. The planning and presentation had to look simple and natural. It all had to be perfect.

"Could we name them after the Three Stooges, Mommy?"

Sparrow touched the lobsters' hard, smooth shells. "They smell funny," she said. "Hello, Larry. Hello, Curly. Hello, Joe."

"Moe," Suzanne corrected absently.

"Moe?"

"It's not Joe, Sparrow. It's Moe."

The little girl frowned. "Moe?"

"Yes. The one with the shaggy black hair is named Moe."

"But there is one named Joe. A fat one—"

"Sparrow, please."

Suzanne put the wine into the refrigerator. She had considered getting champagne, but it hadn't seemed worth the cost of a good bottle. A Pouilly-Fuissé, properly chilled, would be perfect.

"Can they sleep in my bed with me?"

Suzanne looked down at her daughter, confused. What was the child talking about? The Three Stooges? Perhaps she was trying to understand who these people were coming here today.

"They're coming only for lunch, Sparrow. They aren't staying for a long time."

"Oh." She looked at the lobsters wriggling on the countertop. They weren't pets after all. "Can't we get something that can stay? Please."

The water was almost at a full boil. She could have bought canned lobster. Or frozen. But she wanted it to be the best bisque they ever ate. She wanted them to say, "You made this from scratch? You're amazing."

"Can't we, Mommy?"

"What?"

"Can't we get a kitten or a—"

"Sparrow, how many times have we discussed this? Don't you want to keep the new apartment clean and pretty?"

"But a fish—"

"The subject is closed. *Fini.* Like they say where?"

"France," the little girl said sadly.

"Right. I am very busy right now. I want you to go to your room and play with your dollhouse."

Sparrow's mouth opened as if to answer, then closed

again. She turned and went to her room. Suzanne dropped the lobsters, one by one, into the boiling water.

The bisque had to have the taste of fresh lobster. The poached chicken had to be cool, not cold; the Brie runny; the chèvre rich; the mousse light. Suzanne had spent almost six dollars just on the lettuce for the salad—arugula, romaine, radiccio. Then yellow peppers, and tomatoes at $2.09 a pound. All that was left to do was the vinaigrette. Dijon mustard was the secret there. She drizzled the oil into the vinegar mixture, whisking it until it was perfectly blended.

Suzanne walked into the dining room. The apartment was sparse. The mortgage payments alone ate up a good chunk of her salary. But it was still cheaper than any she had looked at on Beacon Hill. And the area was up and coming. The waterfront renovation had been written up in *Time* magazine. Her colleagues marveled at her good investment.

She placed some irises in a clear vase in the center of the glass and chrome table. The table was set for three, blue linen napkins folded in the shape of a fan, their bottoms held together by clear glass holders. Someday she would have Waterford crystal and Rosenthal china. For now, the clear glass she used seemed a deliberate choice, made the sparseness of the apartment seem right.

The only thing now was dressing Sparrow and herself. Suzanne checked her watch. Her guests would be here in thirty minutes. She wanted to seem relaxed and put together when they arrived. Perhaps she would even be sitting and sipping a glass of wine. Yes. That would be perfect.

Suzanne went to Sparrow's room. One corner was dominated by a large Victorian-style dollhouse. The little dolls who lived inside had miniature Victorian furniture—

tiny fringed lamps and floral rugs and overstuffed chairs. The lights turned on and off. Sometimes, as Sparrow slept, Suzanne would turn the little lights on and peer inside at the inanimate family that lived there, frozen in their small beds or posed at their ornate dining room table, eating an imaginary dinner. Sometimes she felt guilty that perhaps the dollhouse had been a bribe for Sparrow to forgive her for all the time she spent at work. But then Suzanne reminded herself that the child loved the house and the little family who lived there, a blond family with permanent smiles and a dalmatian whose tail was forever in the upward swing of a wag. Besides, it was a good investment.

Sparrow sat in front of it now, rearranging the living room furniture.

"The daddy wants his chair near the fireplace for winter," she explained when her mother walked in.

Suzanne looked inside. It didn't look right, all the furniture lined up against the wall like that. The chair should be by the window and the couch in front of the fireplace. But she nodded anyway. Later, maybe tomorrow, she would switch it all back.

"Are you ready to put on your pretty pink dress for the company?"

"Yes," Sparrow said. She got up reluctantly and began to undress.

"Now, remember, you'll play chopsticks on the piano when I ask you to. Can you play it without any mistakes?"

Sparrow nodded.

"Then you can get your special plate from the refrigerator and eat your lunch in here so the ladies can have a nice visit without any interruptions. All right?"

Suzanne slipped the dress over the girl's head and buttoned the tiny white buttons on the back.

"Is it my bunny plate?"

"Yes. So you must be what?"

"Very, very careful."

"That's right." The Wedgwood child's set painted with Beatrix Potter rabbits had been a gift for Sparrow from Suzanne's new boss last Christmas.

"Now, let me see you."

The little girl turned around obediently.

"You look so pretty. Put on your white tights and these shoes while I get dressed."

And thirty minutes later Sparrow sat on the couch that overlooked Boston Harbor sipping milk from a Wedgwood cup while her mother sat beside her in a pale blue silk dress, a glass of chilled Pouilly-Fuissé in her hand.

The buzzer sounded. Claudia and Elizabeth were here.

"Let's bring the cheapest Chianti we can find," Claudia had said.

She had always loved liquor stores, the bottles lined up in perfect order, like books in a library. She ran her fingers over the glass as she walked behind Elizabeth toward a swaying sign: WINE. Her fingers touched scotch, vermouth, vodka.

"I don't know. She's a big executive now." Elizabeth stood in front of CALIFORNIA WINES. "These seem right somehow. Nouveau wine."

"No. I'm telling you, she'll die laughing if we give her a cheap Chianti like the ones we used to guzzle in school."

Elizabeth smiled. "The stories those bottles could tell."

"How many of these did we drink in those days?" Claudia held up a bottle of $2.99 Chianti. "What do you say?"

"What the hell?" Elizabeth laughed. "Get two."

Claudia had been trying for months to get them together. Just the three of them. We're neighbors now, she had told Suzanne over the telephone. Ninety miles down the pike and you can be in rural bliss, laughing about old times. Perhaps sometime soon, Suzanne usually said. It was Elizabeth who suggested that maybe Suzanne didn't want to see them. Are you crazy? Claudia had laughed. Who else can remind her of the time that Abel stood up in class and read his essay about the most beautiful thing he'd ever seen?

Now they were heading east on Route 90 in their dusty red pickup truck, two bottles of Chianti wedged between them. Elizabeth drove.

"Remember that time we went to the all-night Howard Johnson's and there was only one waitress?" Claudia said. "The place was packed and she just couldn't handle all those people? I started making sundaes and you brought them to the tables."

"Suzanne kept saying, 'We're going to get in trouble.' "

"We had to convince her to do everything. She had the potential to be very uptight."

"We sort of had to convince her to get together today," Elizabeth said.

"It's just that she's so busy with this new job and everything. And Sparrow."

The leaves were just beginning to turn colors. Here and there was a yellow leaf. A few red ones. But as they neared Boston, the trees were all dark green.

"Newton," Claudia announced. She had read the toll card the entire way. As they passed a town she would find it on the card, then read all the towns still to come.

"This is it," Claudia said. "Boston's coming right up."

"You know," Elizabeth said, "maybe we shouldn't talk too much about the past."

"What do you mean? That's what brought us together, that's who we are."

"But Suzanne may not want to talk about Abel."

Claudia studied the directions she had neatly written down. She had everything organized. Maps, directions, change for the tolls.

"Did she ever tell you what happened between them?" Claudia asked without looking up.

"What's there to tell?"

"The details," Claudia said.

"That's what I mean. She doesn't like to talk about it."

"Maybe she needs to." Claudia looked out the window. "That's it. The one closest to the water." She pointed to two tall towers, slabs of concrete with evenly spaced windows and balconies.

When they got out of the truck, Claudia said, "We made over forty dollars that night."

"What night?"

"At Howard Johnson's. Remember what we talked about before we went there? We were up in our room, drinking wine, and we told each other our deepest secrets. Remember?"

Elizabeth put her arm around her friend. "We took that money and bought lobsters. The next night we took them to Suzanne and Abel's and cooked them on the beach."

"Suzanne was the only one who knew all the words to 'Puff the Magic Dragon.' She sang the entire song that night."

That was the image Claudia held as they walked toward the tower overlooking the bay—Suzanne's face in the light of the fire they'd built on the beach that night, her hair hanging past her shoulders, hugging herself in an old green sweater of Abel's. Behind her the waves beat the shore and the smell of salt and lobster was thick. "And then one day it happened/Jackie Paper came no more/And Puff that fearless dragon/He ceased his mighty roar." Suzanne's voice had been clear and low, just loud enough to be heard above the ocean behind them.

Claudia hummed the tune now, softly. She still didn't know all the words.

The streets around Elizabeth and Howard's loft on Broome Street had been filled with Italians—old men and women sitting on the stoops, children playing on the sidewalks, spilling into the street. The hallways always smelled of garlic and sausage. Beneath their open windows, the city had shouted.

Here, at Suzanne's, there was no noise. The hushed tones the doorman spoke in, the soundless elevator that whisked them up to the nineteenth floor, made Elizabeth feel as if she were in a tomb. The walls and carpets of the lobby and hallway were muted grays and tans, and the air smelled like a vacuum cleaner. The doorbell Claudia pushed sent a single low cry into the apartment.

It had been over three years since Elizabeth had seen Suzanne. The woman who opened the door seemed like an older sister to the girl she had known. Her hair was chin-length, evenly cut, and unnaturally highlighted. Elizabeth's mind flashed to a hysterical Suzanne, her long hair soaked with tears and sweat, her eyes puffy, red blotches on her face. "Peter married Claudia," she had cried. "But Abel doesn't want me. He doesn't want our baby."

"Well, you two haven't changed at all," Suzanne said brusquely.

The frightened girl had vanished. Elizabeth focused on the women in front of her.

Claudia laughed, a sharp nervous laugh that pierced all the silence around them.

"I know," Claudia said, "long hair went out last year, right?"

Suzanne blinked at them as if in too-bright lighting, then led them inside, her high heels clicking across the parquet floors. They walked through a nearly empty foyer and into the expansive room that served as both dining room and living room. There was a sweeping view of Boston Harbor and, across it, Logan Airport.

"Wow!" Claudia said. "Beachfront property."

Blink. Blink.

Elizabeth cleared her throat. "This is lovely. Really lovely."

No one noticed the little girl in the pink dress sitting on the couch, her feet sticking straight out, her hands folded, until Suzanne pointed toward her.

"Sparrow," she said.

As if on command, the little girl rose and started to walk toward them. She hesitated until her mother said, "Yes," then came over to them.

"This is Claudia and Elizabeth."

"How do you do?" Sparrow said. She looked at her mother for approval.

Suzanne nodded.

"You should see where we live," Claudia said, bending down to the little girl's height. "On a farm."

"With animals?"

"No animals. But there's a big barn and a pond. Can you swim, Sparrow?"

"I don't know."

"Of course you know, Sparrow," Suzanne said sharply.

The little girl frowned.

"I have a big boy named Simon. He could teach you.

151

He taught Elizabeth's little girl, and she's as big as you. Would you like to come visit us and learn to swim?"

"She had instruction this summer," Suzanne said. "Formal instruction. Didn't you, Sparrow?"

"We blew bubbles in the pool."

"And kicked your feet as well."

Silence.

Silence until Suzanne said, "Are you ready to play for the ladies?"

Sparrow walked to the white baby grand piano, climbed onto the stool, and played her rehearsed piece.

"Bravo!" Claudia said when she finished.

"Play something else for us," Elizabeth said.

Sparrow looked at her mother.

"It's time to do what now?" Suzanne said. "What did we discuss?"

"Time to eat."

"And let the ladies what?"

"Have a nice visit."

"There's plenty of time for that," Claudia said, and sat beside her at the piano. "Can you play this?" Slowly, Claudia picked out the melody to 'Puff the Magic Dragon.' "Your mommy knows the words. Come on, Suzanne."

"Do you, Mommy?"

In that instant, Suzanne was flooded with memories. She thought she could embrace her old friends and draw them into her life again. But the memories were too full of Abel, of failures, for that. Had she worked this hard to let all of that back in? For a moment, she smelled the salty Maine air. She exhaled to release it. The past, these friendships, had to stay behind her.

"Sparrow, you may get your plate now," Suzanne said.

The little girl opened her mouth, then closed it again quickly.

"Nice little robot you've got there," Claudia said after Sparrow left the room.

"She's lovely," Elizabeth said quickly. "Very lovely." How many times have I said lovely? Elizabeth wondered.

The three women looked at one another.

Claudia laughed, loud and shaky. "We almost forgot the wine!"

She handed the bag to Suzanne. "Don't be embarrassed," she smiled. "It was the least we can do."

Suzanne pulled out the bottles, blinked.

"You've entered a totally new dimension," Claudia said in her best Rod Serling voice, after humming the beginning of the *Twilight Zone* opening, "the 1960's zone! Suzanne thought she was in the seventies, but suddenly strange things began to happen to her. 'Puff the Magic Dragon' played on the piano. Women with long hair showed up on her doorstep. And cheap Chianti appeared in her hand. Without realizing it, Suzanne had stepped into the sixties zone."

Elizabeth laughed until she looked at Suzanne, who smiled politely, then said, "Well, I think I'll return to the present and get us a little Pouilly-Fuissé. Excuse me."

"I thought it was funny," Elizabeth said when they were alone.

"Maybe I shouldn't have made that robot comment."

When Suzanne returned with the wine, they sat on the couch facing her, and the water beyond the window. Claudia produced a snapshot.

"Here's our crew," she said, and handed it to Suzanne.

It was a picture of the boys and Rebekah. Simon is holding up two fingers like horns behind Henry's head. Sitting in front of them is Rebekah, frowning into the camera.

Claudia waited for Suzanne's facade to crack. In a way, she seemed more like that college girl with the music box and stuffed animals. What about all those nights we talked in the dark? Claudia thought. In the same way Claudia clung to the past, she saw that Suzanne had severed it. Sadly, she took the picture back and looked right into her old friend's eyes. Remember all my yearning, my wondering, Claudia thought, as if the words could somehow reach Suzanne. This is what filled it, these little boys. But Suzanne averted her gaze and stood up.

They moved, stiffly and silently, to the dining area.

"Oh, no," Suzanne said as she placed the platter of chicken on the table. "I hope you're over that vegetarian thing, Elizabeth."

"I haven't eaten meat since I was seventeen, Suzanne. I would hardly call that a thing."

Claudia laughed loudly.

"At least you can eat the bisque," Suzanne said.

They did. Silently.

Elizabeth thought there was something funereal in the silence. She had felt that day Suzanne abruptly walked out of her loft in New York that their friendship had somehow changed forever. Seeing her today, Elizabeth realized that Suzanne had to let the three of them go to move forward. And as her friend, Elizabeth had to let her go, to let her put those days in Maine behind her.

"I made it from scratch," Suzanne said as she cleared the dishes. "Fresh lobster."

Claudia smiled. "Speaking of lobsters, Elizabeth and I were just talking about that night we ate lobster on the beach? Remember?"

She waited for an answer, but when no one spoke, she went on. "Do you remember how we got the money for those lobsters?"

"I barely remember the evening."

Elizabeth cleared her throat.

154

"Barely recall the evening? Before we left, Elizabeth was in our room and we—"

"What a lovely salad," Elizabeth said.

"Thank you. You know, the thing about that bisque is that I used fresh lobster meat."

"Lobster," Claudia said, "is exactly what we bought with those tips. We cooked them on the beach in front of Abel's, for God's sake. We built a big fire right there on the beach."

Suzanne blinked her bright-light blink.

"Well," Elizabeth said, "everything looks really beautiful."

"Thank you," Suzanne said.

"It was," Claudia said, "the best lobster I ever ate."

CLAUDIA, 1979

The last thing Peter gave Claudia was a bird. A lime green parakeet in an antique silver cage. And when she let it go, when she opened the cage and let it perch on her finger, blinking and cooing at her, when she brought it upstairs and opened the window and released it, she let them all go—the boys and Peter and the little parakeet. It was the only way. Until the day she and Johnathan left the farm, the cage stood in the living room, dusty and blackened and empty.

There had never been love between Peter and Claudia. At least not like the love Elizabeth had with Howard or even like Suzanne and Abel had. Claudia knew that when she had gone to Peter and told him she was pregnant and he was the father, he had not believed her. He just looked at her and she knew that he thought the baby could be almost anyone's. He had been a drifter, in Maine helping out on a friend's dairy farm. Unlike the boys she had known back home, or the ones she met at college, or the professor who promised her he'd leave his wife soon, Peter frightened her with his intense stare and quick temper. He frightened her in a way that drew her to him. She would skip classes and go to his friend's farm to meet him and they would make love to the sound of cows mooing, with the smell of manure and hay all around them.

The first night they met, at a bar full of locals dancing to banjo music, songs like "Oh! Susannah" and "Camptown Races," he had taken her fiercely in the parking lot, the gravel making tiny red dents in her knees. Later, back inside, she stood on one of the wooden tables and drank beer from a pitcher and tequila straight from the bottle as he stood beneath her, roughly clutching her calves and staring at her hard.

The baby was his and she knew it and she didn't care if he believed her. In fact, it wasn't until Simon had emerged from her, bald and bloody but even then with his father's angular face, that Peter believed her and, perhaps, started to love her just a little. And with each blond boy she gave him, he loved her a little more, gazed at her in awe as if she alone had created them, as if their strong lovemaking had nothing to do with these babies at all. She would tell him each time, "Look what you gave me," but he would shake his own blond head and touch the baby's fingers and toes, amazed.

The last thing he gave her was the parakeet in the silver cage. Peter brought it home one day after Claudia had had an episode at the pond. That's what he called them, episodes. "Your mother had an episode last night," he would tell Johnathan and Henry. And then the boys began to say it too. "Hurry! Mom's having an episode at the pond."

"Look what I have for you," he told her when he brought the bird home. This was before he sold copy machines, when he was trying to work the farm alone, after Howard had left.

Peter set the stand up and put the cage on top of it, then pulled off the little green cloth that was over it. The bird tucked its head under its wing.

Claudia walked up to the cage. For an instant, Peter was afraid she would hurt the little bird. But she walked right up to the cage, stuck her finger in between the bars, and said, "Hello, Polly. Hello."

No one ever called it Polly except for Claudia. Everyone else had their own name for it. Shakespeare. Gatsby. Alcatraz.

Johnathan would take the bird into his room and let it perch on his head. They would whistle together, Johnathan able to duplicate the bird's shrill sound.

"Don't get too attached to Polly," Claudia would warn him. "You can never tell when someone will leave."

"You won't leave me, Shakespeare, will you?"

The little green parakeet would just cock its head.

For a time Claudia had done graduate work at the University of Massachusetts. She'd uprooted all of them—Peter, Simon, and Henry—and moved the whole family to Western Massachusetts, where they'd lived in a series of second-floor apartments in two-family houses. Everyone had left Maine. Suzanne had gone to Boston and Elizabeth to New York. She'd had to move on too. But at night, as Peter paced the slanted wooden floors, Claudia knew that this wasn't right, and she would lay in bed and try to devise a new plan.

It wasn't until she was pregnant with Johnathan that she thought of buying the farm. Elizabeth wrote her long letters from New York about the city stifling her creativity. "When Howard gets back," she wrote, "we'll start a new life somewhere. We want Rebekah to grow up free, for her to look up at night and see the stars."

Peter had no real ambition. He never did. Instead, he worked at various jobs—carpentry, roofing, whatever came along. He always spoke fondly of his time in Maine, helping out on his friend's farm. "That's real work," he would say. And so Claudia drove little back roads of the Berkshires, through towns with names like Florence and Chester, singing "99 Bottles of Beer" with Simon. Until one day she found it, a farm with a crab apple tree in bloom and a clump of tall daisies in front of the house. By this time Johnathan was born and she sat on a tree that had fallen in a storm, the baby on her back, watching the two older boys run over the sloping land, and she knew that, finally, she had found them all a home.

Peter wasn't enough. That was what Claudia knew. He was big and blond and made fierce love to her, biting her shoulders and tugging her hair. But alone at night, in that time between dinner and bed, with the boys already asleep and darkness all around, the only thing they could do was stare at one another. Sometimes, if she was enrolled in a class, Claudia would explain a battle she was studying and Peter would look at her without expression. Ancient Greece meant nothing to him. "It's such a waste of time," he would say sometimes. But usually he remained silent. What had they talked about before they were married? Claudia would wonder. Surely they had spoken, laughed, argued. But all she could remember was the smell of the farm as they made love in the tall scratchy grass. The only laughter she could recall was that of the others around them, crammed into Abel's van looking for adventures.

And so she knew that getting a farm and gathering everyone back together was her only hope. She tried to explain this to Suzanne, all of it—the silent evenings, the descriptions of battles fought in ancient Greece. When the two women had been roommates, Claudia would tell Suzanne everything. No detail had been too small to repeat, no secret too private to keep from her. She would sneak into the room after curfew and wake up Suzanne and whisper in the dark to her. Still groggy and wrapped in a fuzzy peach bathrobe, Suzanne would listen and talk until the sun came up. More than once, unable to regain entry into the locked dormitory, Suzanne would help Claudia back inside, then shake at the thought of getting caught. But now, Suzanne had no time. Not for secrets or fears. "I have a meeting," she would say abruptly. "But—" Claudia would say, "remember the time you had a midterm and I needed to talk. I thought I had VD or something and I was crazy the whole night waiting for the results. And you stayed up with me and took the test late. You told the professor your grandmother died. Remember?" "I remember, Claudia, but I have no time right now."

Later, after Simon died, it still seemed right to talk to Suzanne. Even though people told Claudia that Suzanne showed up at the funeral as if she had just left an Elizabeth Arden salon, her hair and makeup in perfect place. "At my son's funeral," Peter said, "all she could think about was how she looked." But Claudia didn't remember any of that. Instead, she remembered a young girl in a peach bathrobe, ready at any time to listen. And late at night, alone in the dark, she would call Suzanne. "I'm pregnant," she would whisper into the phone, "and Peter's the father. Peter from the farm. You know." And Suzanne would sigh. "I work, you know, Claudia. I get up at six. If you want to talk about Simon, we'll set up a time. But right now you're not making any sense and it's very late."

Claudia would laugh. "Talk about Simon? Simon is fine and there's nothing to say about that."

Peter told her to stop calling Suzanne. "Don't bother her with this," he said.

"You just don't understand about friends," Claudia said.

Once, during an argument, Peter told her that Suzanne was probably glad Simon died. "I did the right thing," he said. "I married you and we had Simon. But Abel abandoned her. He called me up and asked me if he could borrow money so she could have an abortion. He said he could send her to Puerto Rico to get it for only five hundred dollars."

"Suzanne's my friend. She wasn't jealous."

"Listen to me!" he screamed. "She called me up and asked me to make you stop calling in the middle of the night. 'Claudia has to learn to cope with this. To cope with the past and what's happened,' she said, 'and I can't help her.' "

It was after this fight that he bought her the bird. Not that the fight bothered her. They fought a lot back then. At least Peter did. He screamed and shook her and cried, but she just sat, smiling, and when he was finished she would go down to the pond until he went and got her and carried her back home.

Before Elizabeth and Howard came to look at the farm, Claudia spent three days cleaning it. While she waxed the floor, Simon washed the windows. He sprayed the glass with Windex, then wiped it with paper towels. Claudia leaned in the doorway and watched him work. There had never been a time when she looked at Simon without being flooded with love for him. She had asked Elizabeth once if all mothers felt that way for the firstborn.

"I don't know," Elizabeth had said. "I love Rebekah,

but sometimes when I look at her I feel more frustrated than loving. When I look at Howard, even if I'm mad as hell, I still feel my heartstrings being tugged."

"Simon set me on the right path," Claudia had said.

"He's the model kid," Elizabeth had told her. "He'll probably be president some day."

When Simon caught Claudia looking at him, he turned to face her.

"I'm a monster," he said, crossing his eyes and curling his lips and tongue.

Claudia laughed. "Very scary," she said.

"You laugh like a kid, not like a mother," he told her.

"Maybe I am a kid," she said. "Maybe I'm only nine years old."

"Ninety years old," Simon said. "Nine hundred years old."

Outside, she could hear Peter chopping the fallen tree, already thinking of firewood for the winter ahead. There was laughter upstairs, where Henry and Johnathan were. And beside her, Simon was talking about, yes, how terrific it was to live there. Claudia leaned against the wall and listened, and the sounds she heard were good.

Peter gave her the bird and that was the last thing. No more blond baby boys or teeth marks on her shoulders from his passion. Not long after that he started selling copy machines. He sold the dusty red pickup truck they had bought when they first moved to the farm. The truck that Claudia had loved. She could look at it and see it full of old furniture they'd bought and refinished for the house—chairs with broken spindles, and badly painted tables. Or she could look at it and see the three boys and Rebekah in the back, all shirtless in the summer, and Simon trying to make Rebekah laugh as they went off to town with Howard and Peter. Then it would pull up again and the boys would pile out, sticky from ice cream, and they would run down to the pond to clean up. She could see Rebekah, frowning, standing alone in the back, still holding the cone with ice cream, bright purple ice cream melting down her hand, waiting for Howard to lift her out. Peter sold the pickup and bought a blue Nova with plaid interior.

For a while after he sold it, she would continue to search the yard and the barn for the truck, convinced this was a cruel joke and he had hidden it somewhere. Until finally he took her roughly by the arm and led her all around the farm yelling, "I sold it! Do you understand? It's not here."

Every day he would put on his tan suit and get into the Nova and drive off to sell copy machines. One day, before he'd left, Claudia thought she heard Simon talking. She heard his voice, deep and gravelly for his age, and thought, "He's not dead. He's not dead after all." She ran into his room, but it was empty. She opened door after door expecting to see Simon, but they were all empty. And her panic was so great that she ran to the Nova, got in, and drove away. She didn't stop until she reached a diner in Connecticut, where she ate a salad, a cheese-burger, French fries, apple pie, and then ordered spaghetti and a hot fudge sundae. When the waitress gave her the check, Claudia laughed. She laughed so hard that she got the hiccups.

"Excuse me," she said—hiccup—"but I have no money at all. I'm very sorry." Then she hiccuped and burped at the same time, very loudly, which made her start to laugh all over again.

She drove a little farther, then pulled over to the side of the road just before Route 8 ended and slept until the sun came up. By then, the panic had subsided and Clau-dia couldn't quite remember what it had been about.

She looked around the cluttered car as if for the first time. An entire other life existed there. Old Dunkin' Donuts coffee containers and McDonald's bags littered the floor. There were copy machine brochures and order forms and commission calculations everywhere. And in the midst of it all, there were love letters to Peter from a woman in Bennington, a woman who taught modern American history there. "I stand in front of a classroom full of freshmen and think of you inside me," one said. "I think the English department needs a copy machine too. Come ASAP," she wrote in another.

Claudia laid her head on the steering wheel, tried to think. It was so difficult to think anymore. She used to know all about great battles between Sparta and Athens, names and dates just a moment's thought away. But not anymore. Now, if she tried to think about one single thing, suddenly her mind was open to memories better left pushed to the back, like letting a little boy go swimming right after he eats and him getting a cramp and drowning, dying while his brothers watched. There. It happened again. She was trying to think about Peter. Something about Peter and a woman in Vermont. But instead, she was thinking about a hot August day when she slept too late. Think of the vegetables, she told herself. First the tomatoes, then radishes and carrots. Get to the pond, she thought. Get to the pond and you can save him.

She jumped out of the car and waved her arms wildly until someone stopped.

"Car trouble?" the man said. He looked like he had been fishing. His hat had different types of baits pinned to it. They dangled when he talked.

"Please," Claudia said, "I have to get to the pond."

He frowned. "What pond?"

She shook her head.

"Let me see if I can get the car to start. You got gas? I can't begin to tell you how many times my wife has forgotten to get gas and runs out somewhere and I have to go and fetch her." The man climbed into the Nova. "And I'll ask her, 'You got gas?' and she'll say of course and then I look at the tank and it's right at *E*. Nope. You've got gas. Must be the battery."

"I've got to get to the pond."

"So you said." He turned the key and the car started, easily. "Why, this car's fine. You can go to your pond."

"Thank you for fixing it," Claudia said.

"No problem," the man said.

"I didn't even know it was broken," she said.

Back at home, Peter was furious. He didn't yell or fight with her, but he looked like he might. He looked like he might kill her. He'd needed the car for work, he told her, straining for control. And the boys were sick from worry. "I missed two appointments. Two. Now do you mind telling me where you went?"

She thought very hard before she answered. "I went out to dinner and then I got the car fixed."

"Fixed? There was nothing wrong with the car."

Claudia walked into the living room and flopped on the couch.

"Hello, Polly," she said to the bird.

Peter would go to the history professor in Bennington. Maybe he would give her babies too. Beautiful blond ones. The woman liked to think of him inside her. Claudia closed her eyes and tried to remember what he had felt like inside her, but could only faintly recall the mooing of the cows and the smell of hay and manure. She was empty inside. Even that sweet memory had left her. Everything goes away. She thought of Henry, talking about college. He would go away soon too. Henry and Peter and Simon. She watched the bright green bird hop around its cage. Claudia got up and went over to it.

"Hello, Polly," she said again.

It wasn't right to keep it, to cage it in like this. The bird should fly free, away from here. What a release that would be! Claudia could imagine the neon green against a blue sky and it looked beautiful. She wished she could be the one to fly away. But instead, she opened the cage and let Polly perch on her finger. Then she brought her upstairs, opened the window, and let her go free.

Below her she heard the car door slam, the engine start. She heard Henry and Johnathan whispering in the kitchen. The sounds she heard were so sad that she sat on the sill, clutching the edge tightly. In the distance, through the trees, a flash of green hovered, then disappeared.

PART THREE

FINDING OUT

HENRY AND REBEKAH,
1985

Henry stood at the bus station in Providence, a yellow rose in his hand, waiting for Rebekah. They hadn't seen each other since the night of her parents' clambake. She'd told him that she was drunk that night and had made a terrible mistake. "I was upset about this nose thing," she explained. But he told her that when people get drunk, they do things that they've really wanted to do all along. Henry had called Rebekah every week from Brown to invite her for a visit. He tried bribing her with promises of a ride to the beach, a lobster dinner in Newport, a ferry ride to Block Island—anything that sounded exciting, different. Now that she was on her way there, Henry wasn't sure what had actually convinced her. It didn't matter. He had one weekend to make her fall in love with him. He would try anything.

The bus pulled up and Henry watched the people get off. For a moment, panic seized him, and he feared that she'd changed her mind, gotten off in Roxboro and taken the next bus back. But no, there she was, wearing painter's pants and a blue plaid flannel shirt with a man's baggy coat over it. Around her neck was a magenta and gold scarf, draped to her waist and ending in a ragged fringe. At first, Henry was jarred by the sight of her, not just her new bumpless nose, but her walk, confident and sure. Beside her was a young man who carried her overnight bag, a large, flowered thing with a broken zipper. Rebekah smiled up at the boy, swished her hair flirtatiously, and spoke words that Henry couldn't hear. He frowned.

But then she was there beside him and the boy handed Henry the bag and was gone. Henry thrust the rose at her, considered kissing her on the cheek. Before he could decide, however, she was already bursting through the bus station and he had to scurry to catch up with her. Once outside, he grabbed her elbow and led her to an old white VW bug.

"It's mine," he said proudly. "I got it for only two hundred fifty dollars."

When he opened the door for her, it creaked and swung heavily until it opened halfway. "You sort of have to squeeze in," he said.

They drove through the city. Henry was so nervous that his mouth felt cottony and his lips smacked noisily when he spoke. "That's the Providence River," he said, and pointed. Rebekah didn't look, and his hand hung awkwardly in front of her for a moment.

"I thought we'd have lunch," Henry said.

"I'm starved, Henry. Famished."

He took her to a small restaurant that was filled with men in gray suits and women with fashionably clunky jewelry and large hats. Classical music played in the background.

"Order anything you want," Henry told Rebekah.

"Do you come here a lot, Henry?"

He hesitated. Rebekah had a knack for putting him down and he wasn't sure if that's what she was doing now, laughing at him for bringing her to such a place. But when he looked at her, she looked back in a kind of pleasant and sincere way.

"Sometimes," he lied.

"How did you get all this money, Henry? I hope it's legal."

"Of course it's legal."

"No, I don't think so. What is it? Cocaine smuggling down the Providence River?"

Again, Henry searched her face for a clue of conde-scension. Instead, he saw the slightest hint of a blush. His heart quickened. She's flirting with me, he thought.

"Not cocaine," he whispered. "Quahogs. Contra-band quahogs."

Rebekah laughed. Her teeth were large and even. Henry began to feel as if he were dreaming.

"What about your girlfriend from the A&P?" she asked suddenly.

Henry shrugged.

"Is she still in the picture?"

"Oh, no. Not at all."

"Good," Rebekah said firmly.

Good? Henry thought. This must be a dream.

Henry brought Rebekah to the IHOP, where he worked as a cook three nights a week. He introduced her to everyone. "So this is Rebekah?" one of the waitresses said with a wink.

"Have you been talking about me?" Rebekah asked him when they left.

"They knew you were coming."

She smiled again. Henry shook his head. Everything that usually made her mad was making her smile now.

They walked to the campus and sat on the green under a tree.

Henry lit a joint, pointed out where his classes were held.

"I thought you were writing a paper this weekend, Henry," said a voice from behind them.

Henry turned. It was a girl from his English class. He had tried to explain *As I Lay Dying* to her one night. "I hate preppies," she had told him. "People think I'm a preppy just because I'm from Westport." Then she had asked him to spend the night. He hadn't. Now she was wearing a purple cardigan with a pin of an alligator with a red slash through it.

Henry offered Melissa the joint but she just stared at Rebekah.

"This is my friend Rebekah Morgan," he said.

"Melissa Emery," she said, and extended her hand. After they shook, Melissa said, "Some more Faulkner tutoring, Henry?"

Before he could answer, she was gone.

"She's a friend from English class," he told Rebekah.

"You certainly have a lot of friends, don't you? Me and the A&P girl and now this Melissa person."

My God, Henry thought, is Rebekah jealous? What is going on here?

They ran into Melissa again at the movie that night, *An American Werewolf in London*. Rebekah waved and smiled at her. "What is she doing, following us?" she whispered to Henry.

For as long as Henry could remember, Rebekah had tormented him. She had insulted him, ignored him, refused him. Henry had spent more time daydreaming about Rebekah than almost anything else he had ever done. He had imagined her here at Brown with him, holding hands, kissing. Alone at night he had tried to call to mind her smell, the feel of her hair, even her tight frown. And now, here he was, really with her. Whenever she shifted in her seat beside him, her hair touched his arm lightly. When Van Morrison sang "Moondance" in the movie, Henry felt Rebekah sway slightly in time with the music. In this one day, she had flirted with him, giggled with him, and acted jealous. Henry smiled. For some reason, he decided, Rebekah had had a change of heart. She likes me, he thought. And he could not remember a time when he felt quite so happy.

The dorm room that Henry shared was a standard one—painted cinder-block walls, twin desks and bookshelves, and narrow beds. His roommate, Doug, was a pre-med student, and had posters of skeletons, the digestive system, and the brain hanging on the walls. Doug spent every weekend with his girlfriend back home.

As Henry and Rebekah shared a bottle of wine, she grew quiet and he began to chatter nervously. He showed her a postcard from Pogo that said "Here today, gone to Maui" on the back. He showed her an autographed copy of a book of poems by John Ashbery. Then he took out an old picture. "Look at this," he said. In the picture, Henry, Simon, and Johnathan are standing together. Simon has two fingers behind Henry's head. Horns. Sitting cross-legged in front of them is Rebekah, frowning.

"Do you think about him still?" Rebekah asked.

"I used to yell at him for dying," he said. "Like he could hear me." He hesitated. "Sometimes—"

"What?"

Henry shook his head.

Rebekah took his hand in hers. "I remember how different everything was before he died," she said. "He always used to make me laugh. I saw a movie once about

Houdini. Tony Curtis plays Houdini and his mother dies and he spends all his money trying to communicate with her. But he never does. After Simon died, I would lie in bed and will his ghost to me. Try to, anyway. I would say, 'Simon, come and make me laugh.' "

"Sometimes I wish I had drowned," Henry said quietly. "Even now. It's like my whole family died when he did and I'm the only one who's still alive."

Rebekah turned to him. "My mother has cancer," she said matter-of-factly. "She may die."

Henry put his arms around her. She didn't cry, just fit her body against his, the contours of each settled into the other's.

"I'm afraid that if she dies, that's what will happen to me. I'll be completely alone."

Henry shook his head slightly. They sat that way for a very long time until their arms cramped and their necks grew stiff.

Henry spoke finally as he undressed her. "I've loved you since I was five years old," he said.

HOWARD, ELIZABETH, AND JESSE, 1985

One day Howard came in from the store to find Elizabeth poring over old photographs. She was sitting on the living room floor, surrounded by snapshots. He didn't tell her he was there. Instead, he stood in the doorway and watched as she picked up each picture and studied it. The room had begun to grow dark, yet she hadn't turned on the lights.

"I know you're there," she said finally without looking up. "I can smell the pottery chalk."

"We had a good day. Sold that gray-and-peach-colored set." When she didn't respond, he said, "The ones with the flowers that look like birds of paradise."

Elizabeth looked up then. She had her arms full of photographs.

"This is it," she said. "My entire life. Right here." And then she cried, clutching the pictures close to her.

Elizabeth began to stay in her room, emerging only to go for her treatments. She lay in bed and listened to the sounds of her family as they lived their lives. The sounds comforted her. Rebekah and Jesse bickered. The telephone rang. Howard's booming laugh floated upstairs to her.

And the smells of life! The smell of dried leaves and autumn earth came in through her bedroom window and Elizabeth would sit beside it and inhale and feel alive. It was when she left this room that she became aware of the life that was leaving her. When she moved among the living she felt like an impostor. In the supermarket she saw pregnant women bursting with life and felt even more acutely that her own was slipping away. When she sat with her family and listened to Jesse talk about becoming an astronaut, Elizabeth began to miss living before she even died. And sleeping beside Howard, feeling the warmth of his body, she felt her own wasting away. She thought of the video game Pac-Man, where big-mouthed circles hungrily chased dots and monsters. That was her body, the cancer gobbling her life. It was easier to retreat now.

One morning she woke up and found Howard sitting beside her, shirtless. Instinctively, she reached out to him, wrapped her arms around his waist and drew her head into his lap.

"I wanted you to know that I gave Rebekah permission to do something," he said.

She didn't answer.

"I told her she could go to Brown. To see Henry. He's been calling and she really wants to go."

"How will she get there?"

"I'm taking her to the bus station now. She's going to spend the night in Providence and come back tomorrow afternoon."

Elizabeth disentangled herself from him, lifted her head. "You should have talked to me first. Before you said yes."

"Well, I told her she could."

"I thought fathers were supposed to try to keep their daughters little girls forever," she said without emotion.

"She'll be back tomorrow afternoon," he said again.

"Why didn't we decide this together?"

"Well, you haven't been very verbal lately."

"I'm dying," she whispered, again emotionless.

"I know," Howard said, his voice cracking. "And I don't know what to do."

He waited for her to answer, and when she didn't, he left.

Later, Elizabeth heard Rebekah and Howard and Jesse laughing at the front door.

"Are you going to sleep in the same bed as Henry?" Jesse shrieked. "Yuck!"

"Dad," Rebekah pleaded, "make him stop."

"I wouldn't sleep with a girl ever. Even if there was a nuclear war and we were the only two left on the planet and there was just one place to lie down—"

The door closed, muffling his voice and ending the conversation for Elizabeth. She opened the curtains and raised the window to watch them go. The fall air sent goose bumps up her arms. Rebekah had an old flowered bag of Elizabeth's thrown over her shoulder. Elizabeth recognized it from their days in New York. She remembered the day she bought it on Orchard Street. The tapestry pattern was worn now, threadbare even from this distance. Jesse ran ahead and, though she couldn't make out the words, Elizabeth heard the taunting tone. She watched as Rebekah turned to Howard for help, her arms outstretched. Howard scooped Jesse up and threw him over his shoulders. Their squeals and laughter made Elizabeth laugh too. For a moment she expected them to turn and wave to her. But they didn't. It was as if she were already gone.

"Mom," Rebekah said through the door, "I've got your dinner."

Elizabeth looked up, startled, from the book she was reading. Since she had gotten sick, Rebekah had ignored her almost completely. At first, she had refused to look her in the eye, then she deliberately avoided touching her. Ever since Elizabeth had retreated to her room, she heard Rebekah quicken her steps when she walked by.

"Cream of artichoke soup," Rebekah said, almost shyly. "I made it."

She put the tray on Elizabeth's lap and took the book.

"*Little Women?*" she asked.

"It used to be my favorite book when I was little and I felt like reading it again." Elizabeth recognized the defensiveness in her voice and quickly tried to cover it up. "This looks good," she said with fake cheerfulness.

Rebekah sat in the chair across from her mother.

"I understand that you saw Henry this weekend," Elizabeth said.

"Dad said you were angry."

Elizabeth shrugged. "I don't know. It seems to me that you may be a little young to be spending the night with a boy in his college room. I don't know."

"I told Dad that you weren't angry. I told him that you probably just didn't care."

Elizabeth stopped eating.

"You don't care, do you?"

"Rebekah," she said, but nothing else.

"Why don't you come downstairs anymore and sit with us?"

Elizabeth picked up her spoon and began to eat the soup again.

"You're getting just like Henry's mother. Living in

178

your own little world. Next thing I know I'll find you lying under a tree talking to yourself."

"Enough, Rebekah."

"I need a mother, you know. Not some crazy—"

"I said enough."

"And what about Daddy? I went into the spare room to get an extra blanket last night and he was sleeping in there. What's Daddy doing sleeping by himself?" Rebekah asked, accusing. "Don't you even sleep with him anymore?"

Elizabeth jumped up, spilling the contents of the tray all over the floor. "I guess you can take care of that for both of us now that you're sleeping with Henry, can't you?" she said. The soup formed a white puddle at her feet.

"I hate you! Why don't you just die already?" Rebekah gasped as soon as the words were out. She stood, paralyzed for a moment, then ran from the room.

Howard had not slept through an entire night in weeks, ever since he had moved into the spare bedroom. He would fall asleep, only to awaken a few hours later in a panic. Elizabeth's dead, he would think when he reached his arm out to find her and then discover that he was alone. Then he would lie there and tell himself that she was indeed alive. He would try to relax, but his chest remained gripped in terror. Sleep wouldn't return to him until dawn.

Perhaps, Howard thought, if he worked until he was so exhausted he would sleep through a night. And so he began to build an addition onto the store. It felt strange, making so many decisions alone—the decision to let Rebekah go to visit Henry, adding on to the store, and even the decision to buy a used car to take Elizabeth for her treatments—everything hung completely on his shoulders.

And now there had been this fight between Rebekah and Elizabeth. Howard stood, cutting the boards he would use as the frame. Last night he had heard the shouting, the door slamming, and then sobs from both Rebekah and Elizabeth's rooms. Howard had sat at the top of the stairs, his head bent, immobilized. Jesse had come down from his attic bedroom and stood on the landing.

"Dad?" he had asked. He wore his space suit for pajamas and there was sleep in the corners of his eyes.

"Dad?" he asked again, and then sat beside Howard. That is where they sat until Jesse's head slumped against his father's arm in sleep and Howard carried him up to bed.

Jesse had gotten the space suit at a yard sale in Otis in July. The thing he liked best about it was that it didn't look like E.T. or Darth Vader. It was an old-fashioned one-piece silver jumpsuit with a faded square drawn in the center. Inside the square were colored circles, although most of the colors were cracked and washed out. All the circles had words underneath them, but the only one still legible was UP. A space helmet came with the suit. It slipped over the head and had a big circle cut out so a face could show through. Jesse had never seen anything like it.

It crinkled when he walked. He liked to pretend there was no gravity. He would lift his legs very high and very slowly as he floated around the backyard or up the stairs to his room in the attic, the suit crinkling the whole time.

When Rebekah first saw it, she asked, "Isn't it hot in that stupid suit?"

But Jesse didn't answer. She was an alien on a far-away planet, speaking a language he didn't understand.

He loped toward her, shielded his eyes from the three suns that burned down on them, and peered into her face.

"Get away, Jesse."

He moved closer.

"What funny-looking people live here," he said. Then he reached out and touched her cheek.

"Get out!"

The alien ran away.

"I come in peace!" Jesse shouted after her.

How many times, Jesse wondered, had he seen dead squirrels or cats on the side of the road? Once, during dinner, a bird flew against the dining room window and broke its neck. A friend from school liked to take a magnifying glass in the sunlight and hold it over caterpillars until they exploded. That was it. That was what he had seen of death.

Now they told him his mother was going to die. He remembered all of those animals, the fur peeling off them, the bird's wings growing stiff, the frozen expressions on all of their faces. But his mother wasn't an animal. She hummed in the kitchen while she cooked and made him laugh and taught him about the stars.

His mother had found him the space suit. The couple holding the yard sale were getting divorced even though they were old and their children were old. Sometimes that happens, his mother told him. They were selling stuff from a long time ago. Baseball cards of the 1962 Red Sox. A meat grinder that had to be cranked. And the space suit. His mother pulled it out of a box and smiled.

"Look, Jesse," she said, and held it up.

Just the two of them had come to the yard sale on their bikes. Jesse liked having his mother all to himself. If Rebekah was with them, she would start a fight and make their mother mad. And if his father was there, the two of them would be flirting and holding hands. This way was best.

"That's an old Halloween costume," the woman having the sale said. She looked like an ostrich, tall, with a little head and big feet. Her husband was shorter than her and didn't speak. He shook his head sadly whenever someone asked a question or bought something.

"It was my son Roger's," the woman said.

Jesse took it from his mother. "Wow," he said. "I've never seen anything like it."

His mother slipped the helmet over his head. "Ready for blast-off?" she asked him.

He didn't know any other mother who knew so much about astronomy. She would go outside with him at night and point out the different constellations.

"We got that at Cape Canaveral," the woman said. "In 1961. You know what came with it? Two tickets to the moon."

The man shook his head sadly.

"We'll take it," his mother said.

Alone, wearing the space suit that smelled vaguely of motor oil from sitting in a box in a garage for so long, Jesse would press the button marked UP and travel to a faraway planet. From Earth, it looked like a tiny sequin in the sky. But it was a planet where nothing died—not squirrels or birds or caterpillars. And not mothers.

Once, while his mother was asleep, Jesse took a strand of her hair from a brush on the bureau. He held it in his hand tightly and went up to his room.

"Ready for takeoff," he said, and squeezed his eyes shut.

He pressed the button marked UP and rocketed into space, past the moon and the Big Dipper into a different galaxy until he landed on the distant planet. There, he gave the strand of hair to the benevolent leader. His mother would live.

A November morning with bright sunshine and, remarkably, seventy-five degree weather. Howard and the children ate breakfast in silence. Before they left for school, he drew them into a hug. "It will be okay," he promised. And he meant to make it okay.

It was late afternoon and he worked, his shirt off, his T-shirt soaked with sweat. Howard stopped to wipe his forehead with the red bandanna he had stuck in his back pocket. He mopped up the sweat, then tied the bandanna across his forehead.

"You had more hair the last time I saw you with one of those tied around your head."

He looked up and saw Elizabeth. She looked pale in the sunlight. Her hair was in a braid and she had her knees hugged close to her chest.

"I brought cider," she said, and held up a thermos.

Howard put the saw down and went to sit beside her.

"What's all the wood for?" she asked him.

"I thought I'd enlarge the store." His eyes met hers. "I love you," he said.

She nodded. "Me too."

"I promised myself today that I would make everything okay for Jesse and Rebekah. And us."

Again she nodded. "Me too. I promised too."

Then: "I thought it would be easier to break away *now*. And then it was anger that kept me away. On Saturday I watched you all walk away and I felt as if I had already died."

Howard looked at her but said nothing.

"I've been selfish," she said, and her gaze was frank and honest. She nodded. "I have."

"We're all dying a little, Elizabeth. But you're the

one who's really doing it and I can't know how that feels.''

"Maybe I won't die at all. That's what I thought of this morning. Maybe I won't die and I'll just be sitting in that room hiding. Or maybe I will and then I'd die without having had your arms around me for such a long time.''

Howard lay back on the grass and looked up at the sky.

"Why are you building an addition on to the store?'' Elizabeth asked, and laid back too.

"It seemed like a good idea.''

"What will you put in it?''

"Nothing. Maybe I won't build it at all.''

Elizabeth smiled. "I don't think we need it.''

Howard reached out and took her hand. He felt, just then, like a bird after it takes off, lifting, soaring, high, higher.

When Rebekah heard the knock on her bedroom door, she knew it was her mother. Elizabeth came in and sat on the edge of the bed.

"Lately it seems like I never do the right thing. But I'm not going mad like Claudia.''

"Henry said that since Simon died he's felt all alone. If you die, that's what will happen to me too. Daddy will never be the same and Jesse's just a kid. I'll be all by myself.''

"I always wanted my mother to see me get married,'' Elizabeth said. "We were very different, but it seemed like the one common ground we could meet on. I was always so headstrong and rebellious. The sixties were a good time for people like me because there were so many causes to fight for. In 1967, Daddy and I drove to Washington for a peace march and my mother thought I had gone crazy. 'You'll never come to any good,' she told me.''

Rebekah laughed. Her grandmother had died before she was born. In old pictures though, she looked just like Rebekah and Elizabeth.

'' 'Where did you two sleep?' she asked me when we got back. 'They won't buy the cow if the milk's free,' she said.''

"But Daddy did.''

"One time, during a college break, Daddy came home to New Jersey with me. When my mother wouldn't let us sleep together, we left. Daddy said no, we'll stay, and I'll sleep on the couch, but I refused.''

"She didn't see you get married, did she?''

"No, she died right before. But she'd be proud of all we have now. I'm proud of it all.''

"I said such mean things to you," Rebekah said, trying to fight back tears. But she couldn't.

Howard came in then. "There's been an awful lot of crying going on in this house," he said.

"It's all right now," Elizabeth said, stroking Rebekah's hair.

"Believe me, Bekah," Howard said, "we're all going to get through this.''

Rebekah nodded.

"I'm the worst daughter in the world," she said. "How can you guys even love me?''

"Listen," Howard said, "go and wash your face and we'll all go into town for dinner. What do you say?''

"Can I come too?" Jesse asked from the doorway, where he stood in his space suit, looking puzzled.

"Well, I don't know," Howard said, winking at Elizabeth and Rebekah. "We'll have a vote. All in favor?''

Howard and Elizabeth raised their hands. "Two to one," Howard said. "I guess you can come.''

"Thanks a lot, Rebekah. You probably wish Henry would come, huh?"

"Just shut up."

"And I'm wearing my space suit."

"Oh, God," Rebekah moaned. "Mother, you're not going to let him wear that stupid space suit to a restaurant, are you?"

"I think," Elizabeth said, "that would be okay."

When Jesse told his father that he had talked to a benevolent leader from another planet about curing his mother, Howard told him it was all make-believe. But, he added, it's all right to pretend.

"It's not pretending," Jesse said.

And then, a few weeks later, Howard told him that his mother was in remission, which meant she was better.

"She won't die now, right?"

"She's better for now," his father said.

"I told you, Dad. Remember I told you."

His father nodded and hugged him. "I remember."

That night, in his space suit from Cape Canaveral, Jesse sat under the stars and waved to the tiny blinking one far off in the sky. And when he lifted his arm to wave, it was weightless and the silver space suit crinkled.

CLAUDIA, 1985

W hen Henry went away to college, Claudia began to watch *Days of Our Lives*. It came on Monday through Friday at 1:00, no matter what. She was fascinated with the intricacies of the plot. There was an evil man named Stefano DeMara and a good family called the Hortons and lots of lovers unable to get together and secrets and murder and political corruption. Sometimes Claudia got confused and thought she really knew these people. She would tell Johnathan all about Hope and Hope's mean husband, Larry. "If only we could help those poor kids," she would say. But then she would remember that she didn't really know them at all.

One day Elizabeth came to visit right as the show ended, and when Claudia opened the door, she thought that Elizabeth was Gwen Davies, a double-dealing lawyer who always fell in love with the wrong man.

"What are you doing here?" Claudia said coolly.

"You wanted to talk to me," she said. "You called me, remember."

"I know about you and Larry," Claudia hissed. "Why don't you leave him alone?"

"Who's Larry? Claudia, why don't you let me in and we'll talk."

Claudia did let her in. She was feeling confused because the woman looked less like Gwen Davies once she was inside.

"Look, I brought pumpkin bread. It's still warm."

"You aren't Gwen at all," Claudia whispered.

"Gwen? Sweetie, it's me. It's Elizabeth."

Claudia stared at her. Memories flooded her mind. Elizabeth lived here. That's right. With Howard and Rebekah. Claudia relaxed, smiled.

"I got confused."

They ate the pumpkin bread and drank chamomile tea. Claudia inhaled and smiled. The kitchen smelled wonderful. Ginger and cloves and chamomile tea. And her friend Elizabeth was here, sitting across from her. In a low, calm voice, Elizabeth described a pattern she was working on. Seagulls, she said, their wings tipped in black.

"You said you had something to tell me," Elizabeth said.

Claudia nodded.

"You know, Johnathan is so patient with me when I forget things. He says to try to put things in chronological order. Like a time line. Remember time lines. They would show how time is so insignificant, really. Like from the beginning of the earth until right now would not be such a very long line. Not really. And from, say, the Civil War to right now would be nothing at all." Claudia held up her thumb and forefinger to measure the line. "Like this. I was a history major, you know."

"Where is Peter, Claudia?" Elizabeth asked.

"He says he's selling copying machines out in Vermont or somewhere. But really he's with a woman in Bennington. He thinks I don't know. But I do."

"Claudia, I'm sure that's not true."

"Oh, it's desperately true. But it's all right, Elizabeth. Because I've been thinking of going back to California. That's what I wanted to talk to you about. I have a brother who lives out in San Francisco and I've been thinking about taking Johnathan and going out there to live, out to San Francisco. It's beautiful there."

"Have you spoken to Peter about this?"

"Oh, he won't mind. He could sell the farm and move out to Vermont. His girlfriend's a history professor. Isn't that ironic?" Claudia smiled. "I've already written to my brother. I expect a reply anytime now. Of course Henry will stay at Brown. He loves it there. Well"—she took Elizabeth's arm—"listen to me! And you have to go and paint your sea gulls. I do hope they're on a nice blue background."

Claudia walked Elizabeth outside.

"Why, you have a car!" she said, and gently rubbed the hood.

"Howard's softening in his old age. He doesn't want me to walk so much."

"It's quite lovely."

"It's just an old thing, really."

"Like us!" Claudia called after the car. She waved until it disappeared into a tiny dot. And then, humming, she went down to the pond.

REBEKAH, 1985

Rebekah never imagined that she would shop in a Hallmark card store for cards with sad-faced kittens or cartoon ladies colored blue. But she did. She bought those and more for Henry. One had an upside-down koala bear on the outside and "Nothing to do but hang around while you're gone" on the inside. Whenever he called, she took the phone into the bathroom and closed the door. She sat on the toilet, the phone stretched as far as it could go, so far that its cord was straight. Jesse sat in the hallway outside the bathroom and made kissing sounds. If Henry didn't call, Rebekah conjured up sex scenes between him and the girl from Westport, Connecticut.

Elizabeth took her to a doctor for a diaphragm. It sat now in Rebekah's underwear drawer beside a complimentary tube of contraceptive jelly. Sometimes, after she spoke to Henry, Rebekah practiced putting it in and taking it out, over and over.

Henry was coming home for the entire weekend. He took the day off from classes on Friday so that he and Rebekah could go out that night. She spent Friday afternoon with Fauna and Li, her new friends from school. Rebekah had gone so long without friends that she didn't even mind that these two weren't part of Sally Perkins' clique. In fact, lately she liked having her own group, where she was the important one. Rebekah was trying on different outfits and whispering details about Henry to them.

"Is it hard when he wakes up?" Li asked her.

"Not so loud!" Fauna said. "My mother's right downstairs."

Li picked up a pencil. "Is it this big?" Then she picked up a ruler. "Show me exactly."

Rebekah laughed and studied the ruler. It feels so good, she thought, to be the one who knows.

As she walked home from Fauna's, Rebekah began to get excited about seeing Henry that night. Despite all the details she related to her friends, Rebekah could never verbalize her own astonishment that it was Henry—tall, skinny Henry—who made her feel this way. He had been there her entire life, right there, waiting.

There was already a little snow on the ground. It seemed to Rebekah like it had just been autumn yesterday, with all the trees ablaze with color. She thought of how everything changed without your ever knowing it was happening. Just like Henry. And her mother. Her mother had seemed fine, healthy as ever, and yet she had cancer. The doctor had told them that the cancer was in remission. So all the time that she had imagined her mother dying, in fact she was getting better. There were still treatments, still a good chance that it would return and spread, but for now, there seemed to be a future. Rebekah remembered once seeing a picture of a murdered teenaged girl in the newspaper. The picture had been taken only two hours before she had been strangled in a park. There was the girl, smiling and sunburned in the picture, everything seeming fine. And then in no time at all, everything was over.

Rebekah's thoughts returned to her mother. When she had taken her for the diaphragm, they had sat beside pregnant women and women with babies. Her mother had looked calm, reading *Good Housekeeping* with a picture of Marlo Thomas on the cover. When the nurse called Rebekah's name, her mother had jumped up, then abruptly sat back down. "Go on," she had said. "I have no business going in there with you."

Afterward they had gone to lunch, the beige case sitting in Rebekah's bag. "My mother never accepted anything I did," Elizabeth said. "Everything was a struggle." And then later, as they shared a piece of carrot cake, she said, "In high school I had a boyfriend named James. He wore a leather jacket and smoked Marlboros. I was absolutely forbidden to go out with him. So every night I would make up a different story to get out of the house and go to visit him."

Rebekah laughed. She saw the rebel within her mother was within herself as well and knew that her mother saw it too.

"Did you sleep with him?" Rebekah asked.

Her mother blushed but nodded. "His mother worked at night and he didn't have a father. They were divorced, I think. And we would stay in his room until ten o'clock, when I had to be home."

Rebekah smiled as she thought of her mother with this boy in the leather jacket. She looked up and was startled to see that she'd reached her house. She paused at the front door. It was quiet inside. She peeked through the window. Jesse was sprawled on the living room floor drawing, her parents sat on the couch, looking at a book or magazine. Rebekah stood, staring in at them for a moment as if they were a family in a movie, her fingers absently stroking her nose as she watched.

When she saw Henry's white VW drive up, Rebekah took one last look in the mirror, then rushed downstairs. He kissed her as soon as he walked in and pressed her against the kitchen counter. "Let's go," he whispered urgently.

"Henry! My parents are in the living room."

"I don't care," he moaned. "I've been waiting forever."

But they went into the living room and sat with her parents, even stayed to play Scrabble. When the game was over, Henry yawned, stretched.

"Let's go for some ice cream," he said casually.

Instead, they nearly ran to the pottery workshop, scene of their summertime kisses.

"Don't throw up on me," Henry laughed as he pulled her close to him.

"Could we please forget that, Henry?"

It was a shock for Rebekah to walk into the kitchen the next afternoon and see Claudia and Johnathan there. Claudia had cut off her hair, almost all of it. It looked redder this short. The back had been shaven, like a man's, the top was short and spiked, a punk rock singer's hairdo. Without all that hair around her, Claudia's eyes appeared enormous, large greenish saucers that loomed over her high cheekbones. She wore an electric blue dress that hung like a sack to her knees, and a strand of pearls that was so long, it brushed the hem of her dress.

Everyone was talking excitedly about a plane to catch, departure times, and where to put everyone and all that luggage as well. Rebekah looked at Henry for an explanation, but it was Johnathan who spoke.

"We're off to San Francisco," he said, and he paced

193

as he spoke. He wore a small black suit with white socks and red high-top sneakers. He and Claudia looked like some strange new wave couple. "I've gotten into Stanford, you see. And so we'll go out there and live with Uncle Ben."

"Uncle Ben?" Rebekah asked.

Henry shrugged. "Mom's brother."

Claudia clapped her hands in excitement. "Isn't it wonderful? Of course, Henry will stay at Brown. But Johnathan and I are getting on a plane and flying off to California."

Rebekah looked at her parents, but they were still trying to organize a plan. Henry should, after all, take Claudia and Johnathan to Logan. Would all that luggage fit into his car? Elizabeth asked. No one answered. Instead, Claudia twirled, round and round, her pearls whipping through the air like a lasso.

"Did you notice," she asked when she stopped twirling, "that I cut my hair off? All of it. And then I took it—and there was so much of it—I took it and waded naked into the pond and placed it into the water, all around me like a lovely crimson gown. Henry came and got me out." She put her arms around him. "I got very angry then," she said, "but I'm not mad anymore."

CLAUDIA, 1985

Lately, at night, Claudia dreamed of flying around the Golden Gate Bridge. Not in an airplane, but just with her body, soaring over it and under it, counting the cars and the sailboats and the people on bicycles. It was such incredible freedom to feel the wind rushing by and to look up and see the hills and the landmarks nestled against them. The Coit Tower. The TransAmerica building. All of it, right there ahead of her.

The dreams started even before she decided to go back there, before Johnathan got in to Stanford, before she heard from Ben, his voice over the phone sounding tinny and faraway as he shrieked, "Yes, yes, come. Bring the boy. Come." People were calling her then about Johnathan. They wanted to test him, measure his intelligence, look into his psyche. Every day he went off with two men in a black K car to Cambridge. She would watch him walk down the driveway and get into the car, dressed in white socks and shiny wingtips, his thick black glasses smudged and slightly askew. "We're going back," she would shout after him. He would turn and wave, his blond hair cut in a late fifties crew cut. He didn't have the slightest idea what she meant.

For a while, years ago, when she lived in the Haight, she made some extra money by reading tarot cards on a street corner. She would take two dollars from passersby and lay the creased cards out on a shaky card table with faded oversized aces imprinted on the center. "Decisions!" she would tell them. Or "Success!" or "Turmoil!" Then she would wrap the cards in a piece of fuchsia silk and wait for her next customer. Some people would demand their money back. But sometimes they would exclaim, "Yes! How could you know!" And in her dreams now, over the Golden Gate Bridge hung a star, like the one in the Tarot deck, with a lovely naked lady holding one corner of it. Claudia knew it was a signal to return there.

Bo was dead. She had received a letter several years ago from a woman named Molly, who wrote as if she knew Claudia. Remember the Wizard? she had written. He found Bo dead, on the living room couch. But Claudia could not recall Molly or the Wizard. They did an autopsy and found nothing—no drugs or alcohol or hidden diseases. He just died, for no reason. With the letter was a Jimmy Buffet album. He would have wanted you to have this, the letter said. Claudia played it over and over, searching for the significance of the album. Was there a song with a hidden message? Some words that had a secret revealed in them? She even took the titles and wrote them on a piece of paper, rearranging words and letters. All it did was leave her puzzled. But the album was one of the few things she was bringing with her back to San Francisco. It was at the bottom of her suitcase in a brown paper bag.

And now here she was, sitting beside her blue duffel bag in the backseat of Howard and Elizabeth's car as they drove her down the Mass Pike, toward Boston and the airport and the plane that would take her, finally, back to San Francisco. She turned every few minutes to wave to all their children, who were crowded into Henry's car, following close behind.

Once, when she turned, she imagined Simon in the car too. She saw him, for the first time, as the young man he would be now, had he lived. Claudia bit her lip and faced forward again. Was there anything worse, she wondered, than losing your firstborn? She had lost her parents and some friends. Even, in a sense, her husband. But nothing had been as bad as losing Simon.

Claudia met Elizabeth's eye in the mirror. Remember, she wanted to ask, the first time I felt Simon move inside me? But she said nothing. Her hands danced across her stomach.

"How are you doing back there?" Howard said.

"Doing fine," she said. "Doing swell."

She pressed her face against the window and breathed hard, leaving a small steamy mark. She used to let Simon and Henry do that on their bedroom windows in the different apartments they lived in. They would draw quick pictures before the steam disappeared. A smiling face. A daisy. A cat. She used to have so many plans then. She would sit in those cramped apartments after the boys finally went to sleep and make plans for them. Claudia gazed out at the trees that lined the highway. They were blurry images, from the speed of the car and the tears in her eyes. Quickly, she puffed on the window again, and began to draw a face. Before she finished, it all vanished.

"Maybe it's time for car games," Howard laughed. "I think Claudia's bored."

She shook her head.

When she used to drive all those country roads looking for a farm to buy, she and Simon used to play games. Henry always read, or colored. But Simon would sit up front with her. What if we lived here? Claudia would ask, and point to a house they passed. One, large and white and set far back from the road, with columns in front and a wrought iron gate, looked, Simon had said, like a castle. "I would paint the walls silver," Claudia had said, "and put a swimming pool in the living room." "I would marry a princess," Simon had told her, "or a millionaire." "Where would that leave your old mom?" she had asked him. "Oh, no," Simon had said, "no matter who I marry or where I go, I'll take you with me."

All those dreams, Claudia thought now. All the planning and planning she had done. It was what had kept her going.

"It's important to have a plan," Claudia said out loud, although she meant to say it silently.

"Yes, it is," Howard said. "It's always good to have a plan."

"Like when you know you have tolls to pay. You should take all your change and keep it in a designated spot," Claudia continued. "The ashtray, maybe. Or the little dent between the seats."

She had always done that with all her lists. "Simon—dentist. Henry—school shoes. Write letters. Pay phone bill." Claudia looked out the window. For a moment, she was speeding down the highway with Elizabeth in the old pickup truck. East on the Mass Pike to have lunch with Suzanne. "Did she ever tell you about Abel?" Claudia had asked back then.

"Did she?" she asked now.

"What?" Elizabeth said.

"Tell you about Abel. Suzanne. Did she ever tell you what happened? I mean, details."

"We know what happened."

"She never told me what happened."

"That's all water under the bridge," Howard said.

198

"History," Claudia said. "Certainly."

She caught sight of herself in the mirror. She had cut off all her hair, taken a razor after it was cut and spiked the top so it looked like the singers on Friday Night Videos. She had done a good job. Maybe she could become a beautician in San Francisco, wear a hot pink smock with her name sewn on the pocket. Betty, she wanted hers to say. She could wear white nurse's shoes and chew bubble gum. She loved blowing bubbles, big pink ones. While her customers talked to her she would blow bubbles.

"I have a plan," Claudia said. "I'll be a beautician."

"A beautician?" Elizabeth asked her.

"Oh, yes. All day I'll discuss the headlines in the *National Enquirer*. I'll paint my toenails red."

"Well," Howard said, "at least you have a plan."

"I'll need some gum, though. To practice. Remember when Andy Messersmith played for the A's? He blew the biggest and best bubbles of all. He was my hero."

"You see," Johnathan said, "it all happened so quickly. The testing. The interviews. Et cetera."

He was in the back of Henry's car, sitting beside Jesse. Johnathan had his legs wedged between the front seats. His left foot moved frantically up and down. Periodically, Jesse would clutch Johnathan's leg. "Stop moving your foot!" he'd shout. "Stop it!" But the foot kept banging, up and down.

"And the really incredible thing," Johnathan said, "was Mom standing there yelling 'We're going back' every time I left."

"We're going back?" Henry said.

"To San Francisco. But, of course, I didn't know that then."

Rebekah looked at Henry.

He shrugged. "All I know is I came home last night and found her in the pond. All her hair floating around her like a cape. And then she tells me they're going to San Francisco."

"They are so weird," Rebekah said. "Your mother. My parents. All of them."

"Stop moving your foot!" Jesse shouted.

Rebekah closed her eyes. She felt foolish in the dress she was wearing, a lavender flowered one with tight sleeves that buttoned to the elbow and a bright purple sash. At home, it had seemed all right, with their sprawling house and the last of the autumn leaves as a background. But they were going to the city. And after they dropped off Claudia and Johnathan, they were eating at a fancy restaurant. To celebrate, her mother had said, life moving on.

"I hate this stupid dress," she mumbled.

"You look beautiful," Henry said.

"No, I don't. I look ridiculous." She sunk down into the seat.

"Uncle Ben lives in North Beach. Near Chinatown. That's where we'll stay until school starts. I mean, that's the plan for now."

"I would rather do almost anything than go out wearing this," Rebekah said.

The signs for Boston were nearer. She was going to a fancy city restaurant in the worst possible dress.

"It'll be fun," Henry said. "We'll drink champagne."

He squeezed her knee, let his hand linger there.

"Maybe," Johnathan said, "it will be California champagne. Mondavi."

"Stop moving your foot!" Jesse screamed. "You alien!"

In the car in front of them, Claudia and Elizabeth turned around and started pointing wildly. Off to the right was Logan Airport. They were there. Claudia wouldn't let any of them go inside with her and Johnathan. She had an old knapsack for a suitcase, and they all watched her walk away from the crowded sidewalk, surrounded by skycaps and people rushing in to catch flights. Before they disappeared from view, Johnathan turned and did a little step. The mechanical doors opened, and Claudia and Johnathan's receding voices could barely be heard: "What a glorious feeling," they sang, "we're happy again." And then they were gone.

SPARROW AND
SUZANNE, 1985

Her mother and Ron had set a wedding date. New Year's Eve. It was less than a month before they were married and he had moved into the apartment. Already boxes of his things lined the hallways. Neatly labeled in black magic marker—CLASSICAL AND JAZZ ALBUMS, ART BOOKS, LIQUEURS. His suits hung in plastic bags, from the dry cleaners. A small painting by Renoir hung on one wall of the entranceway. The flowers in it looked like colored dots, they were so tiny.

"Mom," Sparrow said, following her mother into her bedroom, "nothing's the way it's supposed to be."

Her mother had had the walls painted a muted gray. "More manly," she'd told Sparrow. The apartment still smelled of new paint.

"Susan," her mother said, holding fabric swatches for draperies against the window, "I'm too busy for this."

"Why can't you just call me Sparrow? Why can't you just use my real name? The name you and my father gave me. Sparrow. Say it. Sparrow."

But Sparrow left the room before her mother could answer.

Later, she stared at her mother as she drank coffee and worked on a client's portfolio at the dining room table. She wondered who this woman was. She would marry Ron and Sparrow would never know her. Not really. She had once seen a photograph of her with her friends from college, long-haired women, one with black hair, the other with copper, her mother in the middle, smiling. When she had asked her mother who they were, she had answered vaguely. "You know," her mother had said, "sometimes we are forced to put things behind us. People too. There are choices we make that change our lives forever." Sparrow had never seen the picture again. She thought now of the one she'd kept, of her father in front of the brightly painted van.

"I won't be home until late tonight," her mother said, closing the folder she'd been studying.

"But it's Saturday. You have to work on Saturday?"

She thought of her mother again, in that lost photograph—girlish smile and blowing hair.

"I have an appointment with the decorator."

"What decorator?"

"I already told you, Susan."

"And I told you my name is Sparrow. I bet my real father calls me that."

Her mother sipped her coffee.

"For the party Christmas Eve. I'm already so busy I thought it would be easier to have it catered and let someone else make the apartment festive. Next year, maybe the three of us can spend Christmas in Watch Hill. Wouldn't that be lovely?"

"You mean we're not even putting up our own tree? Is that what you mean?" Everything familiar was slipping away. Sparrow thought of the decorations she'd made

203

through the years in school and at camp, dough angels and cardboard Santas. They were wrapped just as carefully as the glass and metal ones her mother had collected.

"When would we find the time? I had a wonderful idea. Everything done in silver and white. White boughs with silver ribbons over there. Long strands of pearls around the tree. What do you think?"

"I think it sounds ugly. Fake."

The memory returned to her, of a real tree with tinsel and tiny white lights.

Once, the year before, Sparrow had looked up her father's name in her mother's address book, a big fat one covered in gray flannel. The front of the book looked like the front of a suit, with a thin miniature strand of real pearls on it and a piece of lace sticking out of the breast pocket. The book had been a gift from Ron, another one of his pricey, useless extravagances. He had one, too, a book dressed in Harris tweed with a pin-striped tie and onyx tie clip. "A-dress book," he had said when he showed them to Sparrow. "Get it?" She had not found her father's name there.

But recently, Sparrow had seen her mother pull out a different address book from her night-table drawer and get a phone number from it. "I hate to hurt Ron's feelings," Suzanne had said, "he spent a fortune on it. But it's impossible to write in that book. The pearls are so bumpy that everything I wrote looks sloppy. Not that it isn't a clever idea, an a-dress book."

In the night-table drawer, beside her mother's diaphragm and passport, Sparrow found the old book, and found on its creased pages inked-out names, addresses crossed off and new ones rewritten beneath them. In the back of the book, amidst postcards and business cards and names of restaurants, Sparrow had found a Christmas card from her father. It was signed, simply, Abel.

As soon as Ron and her mother left, Sparrow went into Suzanne's bedroom right to the night-table drawer, where she knew the address book was, and took the card out. At first, all she could do was stare at the envelope. It made her dizzy, seeing his name and address right there in front of her, and she had to sit on the edge of the bed. The smell of Chanel No. 5 in the room was very strong. Sparrow called information in Maine and got her father's phone number but didn't write it down and it slipped her mind as soon as she hung up the phone. She looked at the address on the envelope again and it was then that she decided to go to Maine.

Sparrow waited two hours at the station for a bus to Portland. While she waited she ate at the Burger King in the terminal and read *Seventeen* magazine. Finally, the bus came.

She spent the time on the bus imagining her father. He is tall, she thought, and strong from chopping wood and hiking. Perhaps he lives in a log cabin that he built himself, decorated with plants and quilts. Sparrow smiled at the thought. The apartment where she lived with her mother had a lot of glass—tables, bookshelves, even the bar. It was decorated in black, white, and blue. Just the other day, her mother had come home with a blue neon sculpture that she bought on Newbury Street. It was placed on the black glass table in the corner beside a blue and white oversized ashtray. "Just what this corner needed," her mother said proudly. Perhaps her father would be standing outside when she arrived, with his head tilted back, like it was in the picture. Perhaps she would stay with her father, Sparrow thought as the bus rolled into the Portland bus terminal. She would sleep in a brass bed and have a large leaded glass lamp shaped like a tulip to read by at night.

From Portland, Sparrow had to hitchhike to Saco. It was snowing. And cold. She hadn't brought a scarf or gloves or even a hat. Sparrow had never hitchhiked before, and she stood on the corner, huddled inside her baby blue ski jacket with her hands in her pockets to keep warm. Whenever a car approached, which wasn't often, she took one hand out and waved it slightly.

After what seemed like a very long time, a woman walked by, jingling her car keys. She paused and watched Sparrow's efforts to get a ride.

"What are you doing?" the woman asked finally.

"I'm trying to get a ride," Sparrow said, trying to sound older and surer of herself. "To Saco," she added, "where my father lives."

"How did you get here?" The woman squinted at her through wet glasses.

"By bus."

"Why didn't this father of yours pick you up?"

"I'm surprising him. I finished my finals today and decided to come right home. I could have had a ride the whole way if I waited until tomorrow." Sparrow was surprised at how easily she lied. She wished the woman, who was bouncing from one foot to the next, would agree to take her to Saco.

"Why don't you call him?" the woman asked.

"What kind of surprise would that be?"

The woman considered this. "Well," she said finally, "where's your mother?"

It was snowing harder.

"She's married to a successful businessman. They don't live here."

"Well, I can certainly tell you don't hitchhike often."

Sparrow smiled through her frozen lips. "I've never done it before. I just want to surprise my father." This, at least, was the truth.

206

"You can't be too careful these days, you know," the woman said. "What with ax murderers, men dressed like women, all sorts of things. How do I know you're not really a psycho dressed like a teenager? Huh?"

"I don't know," Sparrow said.

The woman studied her carefully. "I'll take you," she said. "I just wanted to be sure."

However, the roads were not plowed yet and the woman couldn't get into town. Instead, she dropped Sparrow off as close as she could get. Alone, standing on the deserted street with the snow falling around her, Sparrow began to think that she had made a big mistake in coming here. She should have called first. Or come in the morning when it was, at least, light out. But she was here, now, and she had to do something.

She began to walk, quickly, as if she knew where she was going. Her hands were getting numb from the cold and her ears were tingling. She could see the headlines now: GIRL FOUND FROZEN ON LONELY ROAD.

Finally she came to a 7 Eleven. There was a teenaged boy sitting at the counter lazily looking through a motorcycle magazine. Every now and then he would say "Varoom," softly, and shift invisible gears. A radio played, elevator music. There were customers in the store, buying milk and bread and cans of soup. The clock on the wall had only one hand, the minute hand, and it drooped toward the six.

Sparrow bought some coffee and held the cup with both hands, to warm them.

"It's going to be a bad one," one of the customers said.

The boy nodded indifferently. "Varoom," he whispered.

"Maybe eight inches. Or more. Maybe ten," the man continued.

Oh, no, Sparrow thought. This was a blizzard. A real

blizzard. And she had nowhere to go. She imagined being snowed in the 7 Eleven for days with this boy, eating Hershey bars and dry muffin mix.

"Please," she said to anyone who would listen, "where is Chester Street?"

The boy looked up.

"I . . . my father lives there and I wanted to surprise him." Sparrow's eye caught sight of a worn gold garland draped around the counter. A cardboard Santa held a sign. HAPPY HOLIDAYS. "For the holidays," she added.

Another customer approached the counter. In addition to milk and bread, he had stacks of girlie magazines.

"Chester Street?" he asked her.

Sparrow nodded.

"That's heading out of town. That way." He pointed in the direction from which she had just come.

"Oh, no," she moaned.

"I'd give you a lift, but I bet those roads aren't even plowed yet."

Sparrow looked at the stack of magazines. "That's okay," she said.

"It's not far," the boy told her. "You can walk it."

"But I don't even know where I am."

"Listen," the boy said, "if you don't mind waiting till I close up, you can walk with me. I live over on Myrtle."

Sparrow had no other choice. "I'll wait," she said. She looked around. There were witnesses. If this boy turned out to be one of those psychos the other woman was afraid of, there were people who could describe him. He lived on Myrtle. He pretended to ride a motorcycle.

"Here," he said in a low voice and he poured her a fresh cup of coffee. "On the house," he said. "You can read a magazine too." He pointed to the magazine rack. "Any one you want. Go on." Then he added proudly,

"I'm the only one on at night. I let my friends read the magazines."

He had friends and a job. Those were good signs, Sparrow thought. She picked up a magazine and sat on a cardboard box full of cat food at the back of the store. She wondered what time it was. Late, she knew. Terrific, she thought, she was going to show up on her father's doorstep in the middle of the night. During a blizzard.

After some time, the boy came to get her.

"What time is it?" she asked him.

"Quarter of two," he whispered. "I'm supposed to stay until two, but there's no one here."

Sparrow nodded and got up. The boy handed her a large pair of man's gloves. They were dark yellow suede with curly white trim and lining.

"You could probably use these," he said. "Someone left them here last week."

Sparrow put them on. The fingers were so long and wide that her entire hand fit into the palms.

They walked slowly through the snow in silence. Sparrow was so tired that she felt as if she were sleep-walking. She concentrated on her feet, which moved heavily through the snow. Beside her the boy breathed hard, now and then revving his invisible motorcycle.

Until he stopped.

"Okay," he said. "Go straight down the road for about a quarter of a mile to Crescent Street. Not even. Then turn left and then right and you're on Chester."

A quarter of a mile? Sparrow thought. How many blocks is that? Two? Ten? A hundred and ten?

"Where are you going?" she asked him.

"I live right here." He pointed to a small white house trimmed in multi-colored Christmas lights. Above them hung a street sign. Myrtle Street.

"Oh," Sparrow said.

He turned and walked away from her. Sparrow wanted to shout to him to come back and walk her the whole way. She watched him walk into the little house. A quarter of a mile, she said to herself. Not even.

She was surprised at how quickly she reached Crescent Street. Sparrow turned left and then right and sure enough, just as he had promised, she was on Chester Street.

The street had very few houses. The ones there were larger than on Myrtle Street, and shabby. Most of them had big front porches and Sparrow could see Christmas trees in every window that she passed. She was struck by the quiet, not a sound. In the distance, a dog barked twice and then was silent.

Chester Street ended in a tangle of trees, all with a thick frosting of snow. Sparrow's father's house was the last one on the street. Even in the darkness and with all the snow, Sparrow could see that it needed to be painted. There was a light on in an upstairs window and a Christmas tree downstairs with small twinkling white lights. A cracked streetlight provided enough light for Sparrow to see her way up the front steps to the porch.

It was then, as she opened the porch door, that the enormity of her situation hit her. She was at her father's doorstep. Sparrow took a deep breath and entered the porch. It was filled with assorted boots and sneakers and jackets. A couch was sloppily draped in a dark green bedspread with ragged fringe. Sparrow peered through the smudgy glass of the front door. She stood, with her hand tightly gripping the doorknob, for a minute, trying to see inside. Then she turned the knob and gasped as the door creaked loudly open. Quickly she pulled it shut. The door stuck slightly, then closed. Sparrow gulped and pressed her forehead against the glass. She could not believe that the door was unlocked, that she had opened it and then slammed it shut so loudly that the neighbors might have heard it. She could not believe that she was at her father's doorstep. She wanted to run.

Someone approached the door from inside the house. She stood away from the door and it swung open. There, standing before Sparrow, was her father. His dark blond hair was shorter than in the picture, and wavy, and he had a dark red beard. When he saw Sparrow he squinted and scowled at her.

"Are you lost or something?" he said. "Do you know what time it is?"

Sparrow stood on the cluttered porch, her mouth opened slightly, and gulped again.

"What is it?" he said. "What's wrong?"

"I'm Sparrow," she said finally.

Her father's eyes widened.

"Why are you here? Has something happened to Suzie?"

It took her a moment to realize that Suzie was her mother. She had never heard anyone call her that before.

Sparrow shook her head. Right now she wanted to be back in Boston, in her own bed. This was not right at all. When she said her name, her father should have hugged her. He should have done something.

"I'm sorry," he said. "You must be freezing. Come in."

Sparrow followed him inside. The house was cold and smelled of smoke. The rooms were square and small, like Christmas-present boxes. Her father led her to a room in back. Sparrow couldn't tell if it was a living room or a dining room. It was lit by a small lamp with a shade that had pictures of covered wagons on it. A cupboard painted a flat Colonial blue held a spoon collection. New Jersey. Vermont. Ohio. Sparrow tried to picture her mother here, sitting in the faded brown La-Z-Boy chair in her neatly

211

ironed skirt and stiff Oxford shirt. She frowned. This was not right, Sparrow thought.

Sparrow and her father sat across from each other at the red metal table in the center of the room. It had a large yellow and green rooster design in the middle. Her father had called her mother. He had given a peanut butter and jelly sandwich to Sparrow and then gone into the next room and called her mother. He spoke in hushed tones. The windows had dark green shades on them and Sparrow lifted one and looked out at the snow. It fell rapidly to a certain point, then lifted back upward slightly before hitting the ground. When the phone call was over, Sparrow closed the shade and sat at the table with her father. They stared across the rooster at each other.

"She's getting married," Sparrow said.

Her father nodded.

"I mean," she continued, "to someone else. She's marrying someone else."

Her father nodded again.

"And," Sparrow began as she fought back tears, "she . . . she insists on calling me Susan."

"Susan?"

"She says that Sparrow is a silly name."

Her father smiled. There were a lot of lines around his eyes.

"I wanted to meet you," Sparrow blurted out. There was a hysterical edge to her voice now. "A person should know her own father, shouldn't she?"

"Yes, yes, of course."

"Well, then."

Sparrow gulped a few times, very quickly.

"I have one picture of you," she said. "That's it. All that you are is a man in a picture." She felt as if she were going to cry.

"Look," her father said. "Look at these." He shook some snapshots out of a bag that he had brought in from the next room.

Sparrow picked one up, studied it. The man in it was certainly her father, looking just like he did in the picture she had. The woman beside him had long wheat-colored hair. She wore faded blue jeans and a man's shirt. They were standing in front of the bright green van. Sparrow looked at her father.

"That's Suzanne," he said. "That's your mother."

Sparrow looked at the picture again. Yes, it was her mother, all right. Slowly, she picked up the other pictures. In all of them her mother's hair is long and wild. She is wearing old sweaters and baggy men's shirts. In all of them, she is smiling.

"What a beauty, huh?" her father said as he picked up a picture.

Sparrow looked at him. He looked sad. And old. He wore a shabby brown cardigan that pulled tightly across his stomach.

"She looks different now," Sparrow said, to make him feel better somehow.

Her father nodded. "I haven't seen her for years. Since you came for Christmas one time. You were so little I guess you don't remember that."

Sparrow smiled. "I do," she said. "I do remember. The tree was so big. And it had tiny white lights."

"You thought they were snowflakes."

"Where did we live then?"

"In Boston. You and your mother always lived in Boston."

Sparrow's heart raced with excitement. Even though he no longer looked like the man in the picture, this was her father. He said she thought the lights were snowflakes.

"I don't know what to ask first," she said.

"I'm a poet," he said shyly. "Your mother used to love my poems. For a time. Then she wanted me to go to Boston with her and teach English while she went to graduate school."

Sparrow sighed. That was it. He had wanted to stay here in Maine and write poetry and her mother had wanted to leave. Climb the corporate ladder, Sparrow thought angrily.

"It was a wonderful time," her father said, "when we lived on the beach in a tiny house. We were so happy."

"Just the three of us, huh? Then she had to go and ruin it all."

Her father looked surprised. "Well, that's partly right. I mean, your mother told me, 'We can't live on poetry.' But," he hesitated.

Sparrow waited.

"Don't you know that having you was the bravest thing your mother could have done? She went to Boston by herself, she knew she was pregnant . . ." He hesitated again.

"Wait a minute," Sparrow said as she tried to put the pieces together. "When did we live at the beach? The three of us, I mean."

"Sparrow," her father said, "you've got it all wrong. I mean, it wasn't really your mother's fault. I mean, the thing is, we lived together in that little house, Suzie and I did. I wrote my poetry and she finished up school and then she applied to all these graduate programs. And she got into the one in Boston and then found out she was pregnant. I mean, we never got married, Sparrow. I didn't want to. I didn't want to get married or teach English or move to Boston."

"You didn't want me," Sparrow whispered.

Her father bowed his head.

"Why did we come back here that Christmas?"

214

"To show me how well it had all turned out, I guess. Suzanne wanted me to know that I had made a big mistake."

"I don't want to be here," Sparrow said. "I want to go home."

"Sparrow—"

"How could you not want me?" she said. In the movies this would be the part where she would run out and go back to Boston. But Sparrow knew there was no way back tonight. Instead, she ran out of the room.

A woman, dressed in a full, long nightshirt, was standing in the next room. Her hair hung to her shoulders, pale blond and thin. It was not until she grabbed Sparrow's arm that Sparrow saw the wedding ring on the woman's finger.

"Sparrow," she said in a musical voice.

"Leave me alone," Sparrow said wearily, but she did not try to break free.

"Sparrow, I know how you must feel. But that was all so long ago. Your father is really a very good man." Then, "He writes such beautiful poetry, you know," as if that mattered.

Her father came into the room.

"I'm sorry," he said.

Sparrow sunk onto the couch, felt the broken springs deep inside the cushions.

"I've had a picture of you," she said.

Her father sat beside her.

"You've had a lot of ideas," he said.

Sparrow nodded. She was thinking that she couldn't stay here and live in the woods like she had imagined. She had wanted her father to be someone who loved her and wanted her, a slim man, outfitted at L. L. Bean perhaps, and smoking a pipe. "It broke my heart," this imaginary father would say, "when your mother went to

215

Boston." He would make her thick grainy pancakes in his log cabin. He would hug her close and say, "It really broke my heart."

It was beginning to get light now, and the snow had almost stopped. Sparrow looked at the man who was her father. His wife with the musical voice stood beside him.

"I'll get some blankets," his father's wife said. "This couch opens up into a bed." She left the room quietly.

"We'll get you back to Boston tomorrow," her father said.

Sparrow nodded.

She and her father sat side by side on the sagging couch.

"Would you like to read a poem I wrote?"

"I don't care," Sparrow said.

He went into the back room and returned with a notebook.

"Read the first one," he told her.

She opened the book and read. The poem was about a tiny sparrow who has to fly away when it is very young. It was not a well-written poem, but it made Sparrow's eyes fill with tears and then, finally, she cried. Her father took her in his arms and stroked her hair. She imagined him sitting at the table with the rooster design on it, writing poetry late at night. She tried to place her mother in this image, but it was impossible. And she could not place herself here either, in this smoky house with the sagging furniture. She lifted her head and wiped her eyes. Her father looked neither like the picture she had in her mind nor like the photograph on her bureau.

Hesitantly, she smiled at him. His face relaxed for the first time since she had arrived. Sparrow nodded at him, and he tilted his head back and opened his mouth into a wide smile.

_____

Sparrow had slept on the pullout couch without a real pillow. Her father's wife, Melanie, had looked around the house for an extra pillow but couldn't find one. Instead, she gave Sparrow two tiny square pillows with needlepoint monograms on them. Abel's initials were in blue, Melanie's in yellow. Sparrow traced the letters on her father's pillow.

His middle initial was *F*, a large blue curlicue *F*. The pillows were hard, and no matter how she arranged them under her head, they hurt. Finally, she put them on the floor.

In Boston, Sparrow's bed was big, with three long goose-feather pillows wrapped in Marimekko cases. Along the borders of the walls, a painter had copied exactly the lollipoplike flowers in the sheets and bedspread and curtains. As a finishing touch, he had painted scattered flowers on the white floor. Just a few, here and there.

"You see," Sparrow's mother had said as she surveyed the finished room, "if you choose a theme and stick with it, it all will work out very nicely."

Sometimes at night, Sparrow had the feeling even as she slept, that her mother was in the room, sitting on the bed, watching her. But in the morning, Suzanne showed no evidence of that. She moved around the apartment, starched and efficient, as if she had been in her own room the entire night. Once, though, Sparrow had woken up in the middle of the night and found her mother asleep beside her, still in her clothes from work. Sparrow had moved closer to her on the bed, and Suzanne had wrapped her in her arms. The next morning, Sparrow woke up alone and neither of them ever mentioned it.

Sparrow woke up in her father's house to the sounds of a snowplow outside. She wandered through the square rooms until she reached her father and Melanie sitting at the rooster table. In the daylight, the colors in the house seemed faded, like an old book. She entered the room feeling uncomfortable and foreign.

"Did the phone wake you?" her father said.

She shook her head. "The snowplow."

"Harry's out there early this morning," Melanie said. Then she added, "He drives the plow."

"Oh," Sparrow said.

Her father looked at her. "It was your mother who called. She's coming to get you. Driving up."

Hope returned to Sparrow. Her mother was coming here. She would see her father, see the desolation he lived in, and take him back to Boston with them. Or maybe they could all stay here, in Maine somewhere. He just needed some fixing up, after all. When he smiled at her the night before, Sparrow had seen the man from the picture. Perhaps her mother would see him too.

"How about some breakfast?" Melanie asked her.

"Sure."

Melanie disappeared into the kitchen.

Sparrow smiled at her father.

"Well," she said. "You two haven't seen each other for a long time. You and Mom. It should be something, huh?"

Her father frowned. "Sparrow," he said. "I'm married to Melanie, you know, and your mother is what? Engaged to someone, right?"

"Ron. He's awful."

"I don't know, Sparrow. I understand why you came here. Maybe years ago I should have made more of an effort. Tried to see you or something. It just seemed so pointless."

Sparrow felt the pain she had felt so many times about this man, her father, return. He had never wanted her.

"Pointless," she said.

"You know, I never realized how Suzie would be about all this. How secretive." He shook his head.

"I don't even know your middle name," Sparrow said, remembering the big blue curlicue *F* on the pillow. "Or where you're from, where you were born or anything. And you're my father. You know, even orphans can go and find out their father's middle name. And you are my father."

Sparrow saw sadness in his face, behind the beard and fleshy skin. His eyes had no sparkle in them. But sadness wasn't enough. It wasn't what she wanted. She imagined them together, walking through the snow, talking about their lives, sharing all the little things they had missed about each other, the kinds of stories families told over and over for years. Sparrow had sat at friends' houses, around the dining room table or in a den, with snapshots in front of them, and listened as the family recalled special memories—a car horn sticking in Hershey, Pennsylvania, a child getting stuck in the chimney looking for Santa.

"One time," Sparrow said to her father, "Mom and I went shopping at Filene's. I was around eight years old. And I tried on this lady's hat in the hat department. It was a fancy one, with netting and rhinestones and a big black feather in the back. I kept it on the whole time we shopped and wore it all the way home before Mom realized it. I mean, no one noticed it all day! The entire day!"

Her father looked baffled, then smiled politely.

"Sometimes, even now, when I go shopping, Mom will say, 'Stay away from the hats!' "

They looked at each other.

Nothing is right here, Sparrow thought.

"It's just a little thing I did," Sparrow said. "It's sort of a family joke now."

He still didn't see the point. Instead, he looked relieved when Melanie came in with two round toaster waffles. When Sparrow poured syrup on them, the waffles soaked it up like sponges.

"I can't eat these," she said. "I'm sorry, but I can't eat them."

Sparrow went into the room that Melanie called the parlor. Heavy green drapes blocked the view outside. Sparrow had to wedge herself between the Christmas tree and an overstuffed bright green armchair to get to the window at all. And then she had to lift the heavy curtains to peer out. Behind her, on the chair, were two pillows. One had a parrot needlepointed on it, the other a dove.

"I can make you something else," Melanie said from the doorway.

Sparrow shook her head.

"Well, then, I guess I'll be on my way."

Sparrow turned. Melanie had on an orange down coat and big rubber boots trimmed in bright yellow.

"It was very nice to meet you, Sparrow. I have to go to work now. I'm a cashier, down at the drugstore."

"I'm sorry I came," Sparrow said.

"Oh, no," Melanie said in her singsong voice. "I'm sorry you can't understand your father. Abel."

Sparrow turned back toward the window. Why is it, she thought, that no one tries to understand me?

A while later her father came to the parlor and stood in the doorway too.

"Franklin," he said.

"What?"

"My middle name is Franklin. And I've lived in Maine my whole life. I was born up north. Near Presque Isle."

Sparrow didn't respond.

From down the road she watched as Ron's gray BMW

approached. When it stopped in front of the house, Sparrow said, "She's here. And he's with her."

Ron's car looked like a space vehicle against the backdrop of snow and old houses. Sparrow watched Ron and her mother. They sat, motionless, for a very long time. Her mother was holding a cigarette without puffing on it at all.

"Maybe you should go out there," Abel said.

"She came to get me, didn't she?"

"Yes," he said.

"So let her get me."

Sparrow still didn't turn around to look at her father, who had changed into his good blue shirt and put on a wide tie with a bright psychedelic pattern, a Christmas present from Suzanne in 1968. Sparrow lifted the drapes and looked out again. They both were still sitting there, looking straight ahead. The smoke from her mother's cigarette twirled like a tiny gray tornado.

The ride up 95 North from Boston to Maine was quiet. Suzanne felt there was nothing else to be said. She woke up and decided she would go up there and get her daughter. She had to claim what was hers. Abel had never wanted Sparrow and he wasn't going to get her this easily. Not now. Not after sixteen years.

Suzanne imagined the two of them together, father and daughter. She hadn't told Sparrow a few months earlier, when the girl had thrust that old picture of Abel at her, that she did indeed have her father's wide smile. Or that sometimes, when she cocked her head a certain way, Sparrow looked exactly like Abel. And now the two of them were probably giggling together, becoming fast friends. She remembered a couch she and Abel had in their little beach house. It was an old thing with an Indian print blanket draped over it, one of the kind of blankets sold at college fairs back then. Above the couch they had hung a matted Picasso print of a hand extending flowers. It was on this couch under this picture that Suzanne imagined Sparrow and Abel.

In New Hampshire she said to Ron: "Could you please stop? I want some cigarettes."

He frowned but didn't say anything about how the upholstery absorbed smoke.

They didn't speak again until they reached the house. When they parked in front of the old house with the chipped paint, Suzanne said, "Oh, dear." And then they sat in the car for quite some time.

Fear raced through Suzanne's mind. What if Sparrow didn't want to come back? What if Abel had read her poetry and baked her Hello Dollys and drawn her into his strong arms in a big hug? What if she lost Sparrow after all?

The cigarette she was holding turned into ash and fell on her lap and the seat of the car. She gasped, brushed at the ash, which disappeared into her gray wool trousers and the deep gray upholstery.

"Should I come in with you?" Ron asked her.

Earlier that morning, when she told him she was going to Maine, he had said, "Should I drive you?" This time, she shook her head and got out of the car.

The air here was as she remembered it, sharp and cold, almost painful. She slipped a few times on her way to the house, her black Bally shoes not able to grip in the snow. Off balance, she teetered up the stairs and onto the porch. There was a couch there, with an old green blanket over it. She fought back an impulse to pull off the covering and see if it was *their* couch.

The door opened then and Abel stood in the doorway, fatter and bearded, but definitely Abel. Suzanne inhaled slowly, struggled for composure. Sparrow was behind him, peeking over his bulk. She shifted her gaze from her daughter back to Abel. Her eyes scanned his face, saw a younger man there, a younger man standing in front of a freshman composition class and reading an essay about her to everyone. And Suzanne felt her heart race wildly like it did that day.

But all she said, sternly, was, "Hello, Abel."

Her eyes settled on the tie, an outdated, too wide, brightly colored tie. And she remembered buying it and wrapping it in Christmas paper with tiny Santas or snowmen on it. Suzanne had thought back then that the tie symbolized both their worlds—his unconventional one and her traditional one. It had meant they could have both of those worlds. She remembered sitting at his feet, wrapped in an old flannel shirt of his, telling him all these things as he opened the present. Now it stood as proof of the silliness of that time and those ideas.

As if he knew what she was thinking, Abel tugged at the tie.

"May I come in?" Suzanne asked. "May I come in and get my daughter?"

He stepped aside and Suzanne brushed past him, bringing the smell of Chanel No. 5 and the cold winter air in with her.

"Is your friend going to stay in the car?" Abel asked.

"He's not my friend," Suzanne said. "I'm going to marry him."

Abel raised his eyebrows. "Yes. Well, you wouldn't want to marry a friend, would you?"

"Susan, are you ready to come home?" Please, Suzanne thought, say yes. Say you want to come home with me.

"I have to get my purse and things."

"Yes. Well then, get them." Relief filled her. She was getting her daughter back.

Sparrow sat on the stairs and listened to her parents.

"You are as beautiful as ever," her father said.

"You look well also."

"No. I said you are beautiful. As always."

They were in the parlor. Sparrow couldn't see them but she pictured them sitting side by side on the pale green couch facing the Christmas tree.

"I did it all wrong, Suzie. The girl came here in the middle of the night—"

"The girl?"

"Sparrow. Sparrow showed up here full of some crazy ideas."

"She's like that, you know. So full of dreams. How could you know?"

"She wants us to fall back in love, I think. This guy you're marrying—"

"I hope," her mother said, her voice icy, "you told her that was completely impossible. I hope you explained to her that was impossible."

"Suzie—"

"Where is she?" Her mother's voice was shaking now. "What is taking her so long?"

"Suzie," her father said softly.

"Don't touch me. Get away from me."

This was not her mother's voice. There was no control at all. It was fragile and trembling, like a little girl's. Sparrow ran down the stairs, but her father was alone in the parlor.

"Where did she go? She didn't leave, did she?" Sparrow asked him.

He pointed to the bathroom. She went to the door, knocked, then went in. Her mother was sitting at the edge of the tub, clutching the sink. She didn't look up when Sparrow came in.

"Are you okay, Mom?"

"Please, Susan. I'll be right out. It was a long ride, that's all."

Sparrow hesitated. "Mom, are you crying?"

"I'll be right out. Please," Suzanne said. She didn't raise her head.

The three of them stood awkwardly on the porch. Suzanne was cool and composed as they said good-bye. Abel bent down to kiss her cheek, but she turned her head sharply and her neatly blunt cut hair whipped across his face.

"Are you ready, Susan?"

"Sparrow," Abel said softly.

Sparrow looked at her father. He handed her a white plastic bag.

"I think you'll like these," he said. "A few pictures."

She thought briefly of reaching out and hugging him but didn't. Instead, she thanked him and walked away with her mother. Suzanne gripped Sparrow's arm tightly for balance as they walked down the icy path toward Ron's car.